THE TILT

THE TILT

Robin Romm

FOURTEEN HILLS PRESS
San Francisco

The San Francisco State University Chapbook Series annually publishes the fiction or poetry of students whose work shows exceptional accomplishment & promise. The 2004 Michael Rubin Fiction Chapbook was selected through an open competition by an independent judge. Funding for the SFSU Chapbook Series is provided by the students of SFSU through the Instructionally Related Activities Fund.

Competition Judge: Brian Evenson

Cover Art: Claire Rojas
Cover Design & Book Layout: Jason Snyder
Set in Hoefler Text
Printer: McNaughton & Gunn (Saline, Mich.)

The following stories have previously appeared or are appearing in the following publications: "Lost and Found" in *The Threepenny Review*; "A Romance" in *Northwest Review*, "Realism" in *Five Fingers Review,* "Terrible Story" in *Nimrod International*, and "Fluency" in *Limestone*.

WINNER OF THE 2004 MICHAEL RUBIN CHAPBOOK AWARD

ACKNOWLEDGMENTS

Thanks to the faculty at San Francisco State who read parts of this collection: Michelle Carter, Nona Caspers, Peter Orner, Bob Glück, and Toni Mirosevich. Thank you Jason Snyder for copyediting and designing this whole project and for extraordinary flexibility. Thanks Kira Poskanzer, Liz Batchelder, and Laura Davis for helping me see the errors of my commas. And of course, thank you Don Waters—for reading, listening, understanding the milkshake thing, and for being so damn patient.

for my mother

"The quality of mercy is an inexhaustible subject."

—Joy Williams

THE
ARRIVAL

M Y MOTHER'S GOING TO DIE. THIS IS FACT. AND THERE ARE THINGS that must be done. Last week she instructed my father and I to donate her retirement savings. The instructions were given without feeling, but now that we've gathered information for her, she's decided we're ready to bury her.

"It's too much reality for me," my mother says. When she cries, the oxygen tubes get clogged and she has to pull them out. Then she can't breathe. My father's gone for a walk, as he always does right before she breaks down. I'm left watching the ocean out the window, trying to arrange the problems into something we can talk about.

"We don't have to do this now," I say. (Or ever. You were the one who sent us on this absurd mission.) I want her to look strong, to stand up and start putting the dishes away.

My mother shakes her head.

"I don't want to die," she says, and starts crying again. She's been wearing the same blue fleece zipper robe for days. She pulls a Kleenex from the box, yanks the tubes, and looks like she's strangling. I stand dumbly next to her, staring at the top of her head.

I've been visiting my parents at their beach cabin all week. It's unusually warm for early spring. You can sit out on the deck without a jacket and watch the waves hit rocks. Sometimes flocks of birds land on the craggy outcroppings. Sometimes you can see a fishing boat near the horizon.

The cabin is about a mile from Yachats, a small Oregon beach town. There are a few neighbors who keep their distance, not knowing what to say to the puffy, hairless woman who wheels an oxygen tank in her wheelchair, tottering alongside it, the tubes pulsing and hissing, dangling from her nose. A new house is being built up the road; someday soon the dune grass will be filled with houses. It will be difficult to see the ocean. There will be dogs and kids and toys left on the lawn. There will be music playing when the guys come to do the roofing. But now there's only sky and sea and a handful of graying wood houses. Crab nets hang on a few of them. Japanese anchors decorate trim around doors. When you walk down to the beach, you can be alone with the crash of water, the cry of gulls, the feel of cold sand under your toes.

"Do you want some lunch?" I ask my mother. She's calmed down a bit, her glassy eyes focused on the bright lights of the television. Lately, when she's sitting in the chair staring at the screen, she looks childlike—it's in the downward pull of her bottom lip, the way her cheeks have puffed out from steroids.

"No thanks," she says.

I go to the fridge and take out a large container of yogurt.

Outside on the deck, I can see my father and the dogs walking back to the cabin. He's got a bad knee and his gait is recognizable from a distance. It's rhythmic and slow and seems to veer perpetually left. He's taken to wearing a news cap, like an old man.

A few minutes later, the dogs, Pear and Lila, bound up the back stairs. They're electric with excitement. They wag and drool and slide around the wood floors. My mother ignores them. My father lopes up, sets his coat on the banister. He doesn't say anything, but goes into the bedroom. I suppose he'll take a nap now. And the dogs will calm down and follow him. And my mother will block out the world. And I will stare at my feet and feel so quiet it could be a spell that was cast over me.

Yesterday, the three of us were sitting quietly on the deck, trying to feel the sun through the wind. No one spoke. My mother closed her eyes. My father gazed at the water. I noted how the deck wasn't made of real wood; it was a weird, synthetic wood—gray like all the real wood on the rest of the house, not brown like the wood would have been when the house was new. And I was wondering whether the deck was an add-on, built when the wood was already gray, or whether, at one point, the brown shingled house stood proudly on the grass with an odd, gray plastic deck attached like a prosthetic limb. And then, my father shot up, his spine a dart. His face spread with excitement. "A whale!" he cried, delighted or distressed, it was hard to tell; he pointed at the blue-black expanse. We strained to see.

My mother nodded vigorously as I squinted out into the blueness. "Look at the roof to the right," she said, pointing her carefully manicured nail toward the vastness. "Then look straight out." I couldn't see it.

It was just the spouting they saw; water in the distance emerging from more water in the distance, but it seemed to make them cheerful for a while. Now, sitting here on the deck with my bowl of yogurt, I think I see something moving in the water. It's hard to tell; it could be a small log straying from one of the mills up the coast. It could be a large piece of foam. Maybe it's a sea lion?

"Hey!" I call into the house. "There's something in the water!" My mother turns. "Maybe a little whale?" I want it to be a whale. Please God, I know you don't like us, but if you're listening, let it be a whale—

"Really?" She hoists herself up and tugs at the tubing. She lumbers over to the deck. I point straight ahead.

My parents' bedroom window looks over the opposite side of the deck and my father, unwilling to miss large life events like this, appears at the screen door with his binoculars.

"Where?" he says. We sit in silence, waiting. And then, close to the shore, the thing bobs again. This time it's gangly, struggling. It's not a whale.

"Oh God," I say. My father sets down his binoculars.

The person glides on a wave, seems to crawl from the sea, and collapses on shore.

"Go down there," my mother says. "David, go see what's going on."

My father adjusts his binoculars and puts them back up to his face. "It's a woman," he says.

"Well, go down and see if she needs help!"

My father seems frozen to the railing. "I'll go," I say. I go back into the house, down the back stairs. There's a strong breeze today and it's bending the brownish grass toward the water, making it look pale and silver.

The beach is very close to the house but it's hard to get to the sand from here. The rocks are steep and sharp and full of barnacles. The woman's not moving. She's curled like a prawn, her palms open, her blond hair darkened by the water. She's wearing white sneakers, dirty white Capri pants, and a pink sweater.

"Hey!" I call from the top of the rocks. I'm only about eight feet from her. My father approaches.

"What's happening?" he asks. He's not wearing his hat and his bald spot shines in the sun.

I squat and dangle one leg down the rocks, then I hop gingerly onto them. A barnacle bites into my palm. My father stays on the grass above.

She's about my age, late twenties, early thirties and she's pretty, with freckles across her tanned face. Around her wrist she's wearing a thick silver bracelet. Her sweater is torn on the side and she's missing one sneaker. The toenails on her bare foot are a shimmery, lacquered purple.

"What's happening?" my father calls again.

"Nothing," I yell back. She twitches slightly, props herself up on an elbow and jerks her head like she has water in her ear. A trickle runs from her nose, gets caught above her curvy lips.

"Hey!" my father yells. We turn to look at him. He's waving.

I take a tissue out of my pocket and hold it out to her. Her thin hands grab hold of her curls, wring them out. She looks down at her body.

"What the hell," she says.

"Go get a towel," I call up to my father. He stands there for a moment, looking like he wants to say something, then he turns, glancing back over his shoulder before veering left toward the house.

She shakes her head, turns away from me and looks out into the sky. She's shivering slightly—clouds are moving in off the ocean. The wind is sharp on my face, through my short hair. She moves uncomfortably for a moment, writhing in her skin, then she seems to make a decision and abruptly grabs the sleeves of her sweater, tugging off one and then the other, yanking the sweater over her head. She holds it gingerly away from her, wrings it out with her pretty, long fingers, and sets it neatly beside her on the sand. She's got a sexy lace camisole on underneath. It's the same color as her toenails.

"It would be nice of you to tell me what's going on here," she says, nasal, bossy. She's snarling slightly, doing the same lip-of-disdain the blond chemo nurse always gives my mother, as if putting the needle in the port is going to damage her nails, as if no one in nursing school had warned her that for this particular job you were going to have to touch the sick.

My father trots back with the towel.

"Here you go!" he calls, and tosses it down to us. It lands on the rocks a few feet away.

She's glaring at me, waiting.

"I have no idea what's going on," I say to her. It's one of the old brown dog towels from the garage and I'm embarrassed to give it to her. "Do you want to dry off?" She reaches and snatches the towel.

"Whatever," she says and pats at her hair. She looks at me as if I've just washed up on her beach. "Where's my other shoe?"

Her name is Amy and she has no choice. She has to come back to the house. We have a shower, a phone. She can figure out what to do. After scraping her bare foot on the rocks up the incline, she walks stiffly next to me and my father across the prickly grass. I expect her to complain but she doesn't.

"Are you alright? What happened?" my father asks her, his eyes alight with drama.

"Nothing," she says. It's a doorstop of a tone.

My mother is standing by the top of the stairs. She looks at me, her eyes expectant. "What happened?" she says before she sees Amy come in the door. The oxygen hisses a little tune up her nose. Amy looks at my mother and freezes. It's always difficult, this moment—watching strangers assess and absorb my mother's display of bodily decline.

Amy's dripping water onto the wood floor.

"Mom, Amy," I say. "Amy, this is my mother, Ellen."

"Hello," Amy says, taking the final steps up to where my mother stands. She's visibly uncomfortable, shivering, and I can see her reservation as she extends her hand. "Sorry to intrude."

My mother takes Amy's hand in both of her own. "You look how I feel, dear," my mother says, smiling the bright smile my father and I haven't seen in months. Amy smiles for the first time. Her teeth are obviously capped.

My mother walks over to the stove and grabs the kettle.

"I'm putting up water for tea," she says. "Why don't you hop in the shower and Nina'll get you some dry clothes to put on." She doesn't look at me when she says this. "There are towels under the sink. And if you need to use the phone, go ahead. There's one in the bedroom."

Amy disappears into the bathroom. I put a hand on my mom's warm shoulder.

"What happened?" she asks, whispering.

"I have no idea," I whisper back. "But she's so bitchy—"

My mom pulls away from my hand. "For God's sake, Nina. She's wet and cold. What do you expect?" I turn to my father for backup but he's vanished into the bedroom again to nap with the dogs.

My mother goes to the fridge and starts taking out sandwich food.

"I can do that," I say, reaching to take the cucumbers. She swings the cucumbers away from me.

"Contrary to popular belief," she says, her eyes are dark blue, enormous, and lashless from chemo, "I'm not dead yet." Her oxygen tube gets caught on the stool by the bar. I unhook it. She yanks the slack toward her and gets out the peeler.

"Go get Amy some clothes," she says again, whacking the cucumber with the blade.

I go downstairs, walking slowly. Is this just jealousy, this foreboding feeling in my chest? That I can't make my mother stand up for lunch? That she hasn't called me dear in ages? The water from the shower rumbles like a flood encroaching. Every time Amy flips her hair up there, I can hear the slap of water against the floor.

It's been months since I've seen my mother animated. The last scan showed the cancer had spread, despite chemo, and though they were going to try one last drug, she'd turned dour and brooding, yelling at me and my father for our worried looks, our bad taste in movies, our overeager willingness to be quiet. Or worse, she'd sit on her upright chair in the kitchen and stare at the newspaper. If you talked to her, she would pretend not to hear you. She was made of granite; she was waiting us out. We'd come to the coast for a change of pace but the change had only been the bed she gravitated toward.

I sit next to my suitcase. I didn't pack much for this trip. A jacket, two sweaters, a couple pair of jeans. I finger my red shirt lovingly. I should have packed a pair of paint-stained sweats. Some dirty socks. A turkey costume.

Back upstairs, I set the clothes on the kitchen bar.

"Go knock and give them to Amy," my mother says. She's cutting a peeled cucumber for the cream cheese sandwiches and she looks different— a few inches taller, her neck straight, her shoulders square.

I stand in front of the bathroom door. It's quiet in there. I knock.

"Yes?" Amy sings. "Come in!" I open the door a crack. She's turned toward me, wrapped in one of my mother's red luxury bath sheets. She's running my mother's old wooden brush through her hair—my mother's brush? Where did she dig that from? And she's got my mother's eye shadow and foundation on the counter, as well.

"Thanks," she says, coming over and plucking my clothes from my hands. She takes the door and, with a smile that's tight-lipped and all eyes, gently shuts me out.

Back in the kitchen, my mother is setting the little sandwiches on her nicest plate. It's a blue handmade platter with distorted pictures of fruit painted on it. I see she's cut up some oranges, too. She's placing them around the sandwiches like little sun rays. A cup of mint tea steams beside it, for Amy.

"That's pretty," I say.

"Go set the table," she says.

I lay out the plates, heavy silverware, tall, clear glasses. We have placemats that a woman in my mother's support group made. They're laminated copies of watercolor parrots. Amy comes out looking like she's hatched from the center of a flower, an oversized Thumbelina. Her blond curls hang heavy around her oval face, towel-dried into damp, tousled ringlets. Her face is carefully made up to look natural. Gloss on her lips. A light dusting of blusher on her high cheeks. Her lanky body does something new to my clothes. The pants seem hung on her, suggesting long, shapely legs. The shirt gathers where she's pushed the sleeves up. She swaggers to the table.

"That's so pretty," she exclaims, looking down at the sandwich platter, the little rays of oranges, the pieces of cucumber garnishing the top so the whole plate looks like a kind of edible mandala.

"Thanks, dear," my mother says. "David?" she calls. "Come for lunch."

We take our seats around the table. The windows behind it are enormous and fogged from the salt in the air. Outside, the ocean does its ocean thing. It's blue and constantly in motion. It's eating away at the rocks, grinding shells and beer bottles into sand that isn't really brown. It's pink and black and red and rust and a shiny blue if you look closely.

My father looks at the sandwiches and for a moment he seems puzzled. Then he maneuvers one off the platter so that the cucumber garnish falls into a hole.

"It's been such a lovely week," my mother says. The oxygen hisses, stops, and hisses.

My father says, "You can see clear out to China."

Amy smiles, holding a sandwich up. "It's pretty here," she says. "You've got a great piece of property."

At first, when the cancer started, we broke down, we got angry, we denied it was happening. My mother would spend thousands of dollars on new furniture, new appliances because she didn't want to die. (How could she die when she had a Swedish refrigerator to pay off?) When she went into the first and only brief remission, we all pretended there had never been cancer. Cancer? What cancer? We had her back and we ignored the past year. It was a bad year, misbehaving. But when cancer reappeared, blooming like a weed in her chest several months later, we were shocked. She'd get rid of it; there wasn't a choice. What did we need to discuss? You won't get any attention from us, we said to her breasts. No way! You're a bad, bad cancer. We won't acknowledge you and you will wilt, the saddest, most neglected flower in the world.

Then we started fighting. My father came home later and later, began disappearing to conferences and seminars. I nagged my mother about her diet. (Cancer travels in lipids! I yelled. Lipids!) I brought home books on mushroom cures, macrobiotics, yoga, meditation.

But now, eight years later, we're made of a bendable substance, much like rubber. Cancer? Yes. Yes, there is cancer. Yes, there is death, hanging its head in false sympathy with us. Tricking us. Making us feel guilty for not understanding how we're part of life's mysterious cycle. Making us feel funny for hating death, for feeling robbed by it. It is, as the spiritually enlightened friends say, just a part of life. Everyone dies, we repeat to ourselves, this is nothing special, the way the world disintegrates; the way she sits there all day, frozen in remorse and fear; the way her freckled chest puffs out with tumor and her breast turns purple and black, crinkling into a dry mound, the nipple eaten away.

And then the guilt turns into an odd acceptance. Mom can't get up from the sofa without almost falling. It takes her almost a full minute to catch her breath. Mom winces with pain when you lean in to hug her. "Stop," she says, the word made more of breath than noise. These things are now normal, as normal as tea in the afternoon, as normal as wind over the water. In some way, we were born knowing this would happen. We're old pals of death. We've gone from hoping for miracle cures to just hoping the sandwiches are good.

"These are good," I say. They are good. Salty and creamy with a nice, crisp snap when you bite into the cucumber. We're an accepting bunch. We take what's given to us these days and we don't ask questions.

My mother and Amy start talking about nail polish. The one thing my mother has kept up despite the failing of everything else is her biweekly manicure.

"They're just perfect," Amy says, leaning over to inspect my mother's fingers. "That color looks so good with your skin tone. You've got such pale, pretty skin."

"I have this woman in Eugene," my mother says. "She's a miracle."

"Would you like to come out to the deck?" my mother asks Amy once we've finished eating.

"Aren't you tired?" I ask her. It sounds like an accusation. Usually, after she sits upright for a while, she has to lie down, use the breathing machine in the bedroom.

"I'm fine, Nina," she spits, nostrils flared. She stands up from the table.

"I'd love to," Amy says. She stacks some plates and hands them over to me. My mother slides the door open.

I take the dishes to the sink. I can see my mother and Amy from the window but it's hard to hear what they're saying because of the wind. Amy's hair is blowing sideways. My mother stands near the railing. She says something; Amy laughs and puts her hand on my mother's shoulder. My mother beams.

Well, maybe the distraction is good. Amy was all smiles at lunch, chatting about real estate prices and how hard it is to find really good sea-sonal fruit.

Amy hasn't even glanced at the shiny black phone, hanging like a centerpiece on the wall near the fridge. Doesn't anyone care that she's just washed up from a foamy, foreboding sea—that's she's wearing a dying woman's blush in a house full of plastic tubing and oxygen generators and tiny, clear syringes?

On the kitchen bar, pegged by the fruit bowl, is the list my father and I compiled for my mother. On it are organizations and programs that are connected with the law school. Her retirement money, which she will never live to spend, can be allocated a number of ways. My father's illegible writing is all over the margin. Numbers, combinations of donations, lists of faculty who would help administer grants. My father suggested that she fund a professorship.

"It would be a way for you to live on," he said. "Afterward."

She looked at him through narrowed eyes, as if a propeller had started up behind them, as if through a sort of wind tunnel her eyes would knock him unconscious.

"Stop rushing me," she said, her voice breaking.

"What are you talking about?" he asked.

"I'll die soon enough!"

My father shook his head, went to walk the dogs.

My father is on the sofa now, reading the paper. Pear rests near his legs, looking at him with passionate red-brown eyes. Lila is lying on her side on the rug near the empty fireplace. I sit down next to her and put my head on her warm, wiry chest. She lifts her head to gaze at me, deeply exhausted, white hairs spreading outward from her eyes and jowls. Then she puts her heavy head back down.

"What do you think the deal is with that Amy?" my dad says, putting down the paper. I roll off the dog's chest and prop myself up on my elbow.

"I know," I say. "Where'd she come from?"

"Isn't there a play about this?" my father asks. "She's going to fool us all into thinking she's one of us, then she's going to steal the dogs. Or the cars. Or something."

"Or something," I say. "Mom seems to like her."

"Yeah," he says, gazing at the lamp in the far corner of the room. "She does, doesn't she."

When my mother likes something, my father acts amazed. He'll buy raspberry soda and she'll slink off to finish the bottle and he will come into my room, bright-eyed and awed, to report that she liked it! She liked it!

But maybe this is the right way to deal with the dying—you like cream puffs? We'll bring you cream puffs. You want to yell at us for renting another movie with cancer in it (it didn't say it on the box, we checked!), then yell away! It's your world, we're just hanging around, trying to keep it turning.

My father puts the newspaper down. Pear continues to stare at him, his eyes little machines of want.

"Pear's so passionate," my father says, looking back at the dog. "I love Pear."

I look at my father look at the dog. Lila starts snoring. The sliding door opens and Amy comes into the room. My mother follows her, lumbering slowly over the threshold.

"I'm going to take the dogs out," my father says, standing.

"I'm going to lie down for a bit," my mother says, walking toward the hallway. I stand up and follow her, leaving Amy near the large windows.

My mother sits on the big red bed.

"Can you hook up the bipap?" she says, pulling on the mask. Once she straps that monster on, she'll be unable to talk.

"How are you?" I ask. She hates being asked this. She's told me this over and over again: I'm peachy keen! Never better! Why? Do I look sick?

"Fine," she says. "Tired."

"The sandwiches were good," I say. She fiddles with the dial of the bipap machine.

"So what's the deal with Amy?" I ask. My mother looks up at me, surprised. There's a weird look on her face—delight? Joy?

"She's a lovely girl," my mother says. "She grew up in Wisconsin."

"Oh. Wisconsin," I say.

"Her father's an orthodontist."

"So how'd she wind up here?" I ask.

"You're so nosy," my mother says, pulling the bipap mask up. "Switch the tubes for me, Nina." In a fast pull-strap motion, she's got the mask secured, the little motor in the gray box begins to sing. I go to the other machine, pull the tubing in. I stand for a moment by her closet. I can smell the perfume in her clothes. Expensive, sweet.

Out in the hallway, the house is silent. I want to crawl in a hole; it's as if something in my chest is pulling me toward my bedroom.

"Oh!" says Amy, putting down the little box that sits by my bed. "I didn't hear you."

She looks guilty. My dad's right. She's a con artist. We'll turn around to get the milk out of the fridge and off she'll go with the checkbooks, the credit cards, my mother's wedding ring.

"I was looking for my bracelet," she says.

"Well. It's not here," I say. "Maybe check the bathroom."

"Yeah," she says. "Good idea." She sits on my bed and starts looking at her fingernails.

Okay, Amy, game's up.

"Your mom's great," Amy says. She's clasping and unclasping her hands. "Such a fighter."

"Yeah," I say. "Thanks."

"My mom's dead," she says. She looks up at me, her bright eyes transformed, full of tears and—

She's got my earrings on.

"I'm so sorry," I say, but it comes out made of rocks. Amy follows my gaze and her hands fly up to her ears.

"I'm sorry," she says, wincing. "I was playing dress-up, I guess." She must be thirty years old. Dress-up. I nod.

"Hard to resist," I say. She hands me the earrings. "Maybe it's not a good idea for you to stay here," I say. "Can we get you a room in town for the night?"

Amy crumples sideways onto the bed, getting mascara on my pale yellow pillows. I'd get so much pleasure out of slapping her.

She cries and then she calms. I'm struggling to think of what words to toss in the silence that's about to open between us, but I'm saved when she starts up again, giant sobs this time, from the root of her stomach up through her lungs, filtering through her heart before exiting. She sounds like a goose.

"How'd she die?"

Amy struggles to calm down. "She drowned." This comes out matter-of-fact. "She'd left my father in the Midwest and was living in some women's colony near Junction City—and something happened, I guess she went skinny-dipping in the river or something." She reaches over for a tissue—all our rooms have boxes of tissues now. She still looks good, like she's made of velvet or suede, not skin. Her tears make her eyes an even more outlandish shade of green.

"They never found the body?" I ask. This is one of my fantasies—that we'll wake up one day and my mother will have vanished. There will be no body, no clues. And then instead of being nowhere, she'll be everywhere, in everything.

"No, it washed up downriver near a farm," Amy says. "The police called us."

"There's Scotch upstairs," I say. She takes another tissue.

We pad up the stairs, both of us slow, our bare feet soft on the wood. I get the Scotch out of the cupboard and pour two shots in the tall glasses.

"Water?" I ask.

"No. Neat," she says, holding out her hand.

I reach over and pluck the list of donation possibilities from beneath the fruit basket, where it seems to have landed permanently, gathering smudges and grease stains. I fold it in half and toss it in the recycle box at the end of the bar. Amy reaches up with her free hand and pulls her hair away from her face.

We stand by the kitchen bar, staring at the refrigerator. The ocean's behind us, behind the window, behind the rocks, dragging water and debris out beneath itself, out, away from shore.

I want to ask what she did the moment she found out. Did she drive? Did she sink to the carpet and cry? What's it like—the first day after? The first week? And when you do stop living only in absence? But I look at her ears, still a faint pink from yanking the earrings out—I think of her drifting on the wave toward shore. And I don't ask.

My mother comes into the kitchen, arranging her tubes. Her face is creased from the bipap mask, making her look even more childlike. She must not have been able to sleep. Amy reaches for another glass and pours my mother a shot. I almost object—she's not supposed to drink. But my mother reaches out for it, holds the amber liquid up with those magenta nails and seems to see something in it.

THE
TILT

I T'S DAY TWO OF OUR FIVE-DAY VISIT TO MAINE AND NICK'S
stepmother, Anna, has barely uttered a word to us though I haven't seen
or spoken to her in almost three years. She sits in the center of the braided
rug in lotus position, her black hair in a high ponytail, her body draped in
a faded, violet sweatsuit. The room used to hold a giant weaving loom, but
it's been moved to the garage. Now this big room off the living room is
empty save a few low benches where candles burn and bundles of leaves sit,
wrapped in embroidery floss.

"Just ignore her," Nick says. I follow him up the shiny wooden staircase to the bedrooms. He's not ignoring her. He's learned to live with all of
this silently, but if I reached out to put my hand on his shoulder right now,
he would feel like a wound coil, the drawing back of a snake before it lashes
out to bite.

The whole scene is wrong. It's been wrong from the beginning. When
Nick was twelve and his father, Gray, left his mother for Anna—that was
wrong. It was wrong that Nick's mother had to live alone in that rundown
rental on the outskirts of town, reading paperbacks and quilting. The
world has continued to spin like this, tilted on its axis, and it's worn a lop-
sided groove in the universe. It can't right itself anymore; it's gotten used
to this angle.

Despite the sun streaming through the skylights and the white, clean
walls, there's no peace here. The door to Milo's bedroom is shut, but I

know that if we opened it, the bed would be unmade, the snowboarding poster would still hang on the wall above it. It's a source of tension—that Anna will not allow the room to be emptied or cleaned. But it's a battle she's been winning for years.

The windows in Nick's old room are open to the garden. The air is a cool, spring, eastern wood air—the sweet smell of old leaves and new buds. I sit on the flowered quilt and kick off my shoes. It's a tiny room. There's hardly anything in here—an antique dresser with an old porcelain pitcher on it and a stiff-backed chair next to the bed. No trace of Nick as a child. Milo, age seven or eight, grins from a speckled silver frame. On the wall is a framed crayon drawing—Milo's, certainly.

"What do you want to do today?" Nick asks. He's wriggling out of his thick brown sweater. It's not really warm enough to be without a sweater but I admire his optimism. The trees outside shine in the brightness of the day. In the distance, you can hear the bleating of sheep, occasionally, the squawk of a chicken.

I used to come up to this big house in Maine on long weekends with Nick during college but I haven't been back in the three years since Milo's funeral. That day, we came up to this room with its views of the road and the acreage, climbed into bed, blind with shock and exhaustion, and Nick told me that someday he would really understand love but that he didn't think he did then, he didn't think he ever really had—at least not with me. Under the thick quilt, his body altered, became solid and separate in a way I hadn't known before. His knees were sharp, his legs selfish. Inside my own body—already still with grief—a deeper silence landed. I closed my eyes and the darkness was particulate, full of spinning shards and gyrating orbs, but my blood and heart had stopped moving.

Nick is waiting for me to say something. He's leaning against the dresser, crossing his arms. His eyes are the impossible green of old coke bottles and shine with a cool, glassy clarity. I could walk across the room and put my lips against his neck and he would put his hand on my back absently and I would stand there breathing the soapy smell of his skin.

After two years of pretending he never existed, the alien novelty of this hasn't worn off. Nick pushes himself off the dresser and comes over. The mattress sags when he sits. He reaches for me and pulls me to his chest.

We've only been back together six months. Nick got a job in San Francisco, heading the archival sound department at the public library. He called me once he knew he was taking the job. We met in Golden Gate Park, then went to a bar, then back to his apartment with the futon on the floor and his clothes in low crates. We drank hot toddies and I wouldn't let him touch me. I'm so sorry, he said. You have to believe me. And I haven't forgotten about the way he left me, the girls he plugged the absence with until I just didn't want to talk to him anymore, until whatever passed between us just felt like a joke, like some adolescent clinging that we never should have engaged in.

"How long does Anna do that for?" I ask. Nick lets go of me and sits up straighter.

"Oh Becca," he says, putting a hand over his eyes. "Let's not get into this now."

"We're not getting into anything," I say, sitting away from him. "I'm just asking a question."

He breathes in heavily, as if a dictionary sits on his sternum.

"This isn't the worst of it," he says. "There's a group that comes on Sunday nights." Outside I can see a car with a horse trailer whiz past on the main road. A bunch of geese rise off the small pond and disappear over the house.

"They channel the dead," he says flatly. He turns to face me. His eyes spark sadly and his lips smirk. Does he really think I can't see it—the horrified look behind the twinkling one that's particular to this older Nick? A mild shifting in the facial muscles that might be mistaken for aging?

"How many are in the group?"

"I don't know, about five."

"They meet here?" I ask. I'm trying to remember if we said we'd sleep here on Sunday night.

"Sometimes here, sometimes at other people's houses." He cracks the knuckles of his left hand. "Let's go get the bikes."

But on the way out to the shed, Nick's father, Gray, barrels up the driveway in his old pickup. He pulls up next to us.

"Becky!" he shouts. I can sense Nick roll his eyes behind me. Gray's been on call since we arrived, so this is my first sighting. He swings himself down out of the cab; he's dressed in scrubs and white running shoes. Some of his neck hair scraggles up around the vee of the shirt. He looks older, as if he's worn a hole in his body somewhere and the water in his skin has leaked out.

"Welcome!" he shouts. I'd forgotten how tightly wound he is. A dad on fast forward, he talks as if someone's put a time constraint on his life. "It's been too long! Too long!" His hand flies out to the side of his head and thumps me on the arm, then he grabs it and pulls me into an awkward hug. He smells strange, like new plastic or the inside of a film canister.

"You always were a pretty one," he says, winking at Nick. Nick stretches his lips over his teeth in a grimace. "What are you two up to?"

"We're going to the reservoir," Nick says, and I can feel his body gravitating toward the shed. Part of him is already on that bike, fleeing down the gravel road to the main road, the wind blowing his dark hair back.

"Oh, no. Come inside and we'll make a pot of coffee. Becky, I want to hear how you're doing—Becky, Becky." He shakes his head. "And Nick, I was hoping you could pull up some chairs from the basement for dinner tonight."

"Dinner?" Nick asks.

"Anna invited some people over." Nick tenses. I step backward into him but he doesn't soften or put his hand on me. Gray fishes a bag out of the bed of the truck. He swats me on the arm again as he walks by into the house.

While Gray makes coffee, Nick and I go down to the basement to find the folding chairs. They're under a bunch of tarps and old paint cans and Nick begins to dig them out.

"You okay?" I ask. His hair has gotten long and it falls over his eyes, making him look younger.

"Mmm," he says. "He put this damn belt thing over the chairs. Why would you do that?" Nick yanks on the belt, and the chairs, which sit on wheeled palettes, roll toward him slightly. "It's like he's afraid even the fucking chairs are going to try to get out of here." Nick kneels over the strap and starts to wiggle at the metal clasp. I hoist myself up to sit on a workbench. Above my head the shelves are stocked with ball jars of pickles and jams. The three freezers whir and hum. I like it down here. It's organized and spotless and there's a feeling of abundance. At Thanksgiving, every dish Gray and Anna serve they've grown and prepared themselves, including the turkey. There's something romantic about it, even if it is a little self-righteous or obsessive, as Nick says.

Nick gets the belt off and the chair on the end falls to the ground, making a sharp clatter.

"Take two of them," Nick says, grabbing three more off the end. The wooden stairs creak as we head back up, into the dining room.

"Thanks, kids," Gray says. He's holding a black plastic pitcher of coffee and three mugs. We set the chairs against the sliding glass doors and follow Gray into the living room. Anna is still sitting cross-legged on the small carpet in the weaving room, her eyes closed, her spine rigid. Gray doesn't acknowledge her.

You wouldn't know it was Anna who planned the dinner. She's still very quiet even after the guests arrive, and she's careful to sit next to Gray at the corner of the table. She stayed in the weaving room most of the afternoon, getting up a couple of times to go to the bathroom, and then finally, to shower and change. She was young when she married Gray, twenty-six to his forty-one. Her face is still smooth, despite the hollowing of her eyes. She's done something odd with her hair tonight, a Princess Leia look with braided buns muffling her ears.

"I lost my baby," the woman next to me says. I can't remember her name. She's holding her knife and fork above her plate and seems to be trembling slightly. Her bright blond hair is pinned loosely on top of her head so that it flops to one side and her gray eyes are as focused as a gun. She's shockingly pretty. The smattering of color in her cheeks looks like a small, ragged continent. "He was only six months old," she says. The rest of the guests are talking about Gray and Anna's recent kayaking trip.

"I'm so sorry," I say dumbly.

"And then I lost my husband," she says. "To leukemia last year." My knife is in my right hand and I can't bring it down to the chicken on my plate, though I want to. A gesture of normalcy, cutting chicken off the bone. Nick hasn't touched his food. I can tell he's listening to the blond woman but he doesn't turn to help me out. He just grabs his bottle of beer and takes a purposeful swig. I set my knife down.

A peal of laughter erupts from the head of the table.

"That's truly terrible," I say.

"It changes you," she says. Nick picks up a bowl of green beans.

"You want some?" he says, handing it over to me. I take the bowl and hold it for a moment. It feels heavier than it should. I'm afraid I'm going to drop it.

"Thanks," I mumble. I set it between me and the blond woman. The beans look oily. I can't think. The air in my chest has gotten thin. If I don't stand up and go someplace where the air is better, I feel like I might pass out.

"I have to go to the bathroom," I say, scooting my chair out. "I'm sorry."

It's awful to do this, to leave her words hanging in the empty air over my place setting, but I don't have it in me to respond. I don't even know what a response would sound like.

In the bathroom, I sit on the lid of the toilet and focus on my breathing. It's cold in here. Nick and I spent the afternoon helping out around the garden, drinking beer after beer, and then Scotch as we roasted the chicken with Gray, then more Scotch as we hovered around the crackers with the guests as they filtered in. I'm feeling less drunk than tired. Tired from the roof of my mouth inward, into the pockets behind my eyes, down in my windpipes and deep in my lungs.

We've talked about death, Nick and I. It's like a secret we pass around at night but don't dare mention in the light of day. Three years ago, Milo took a gun out of the gun cabinet and went outside to shoot at the geese. He was fourteen years old. No one knows what happened exactly; no one was here to see it. But when Anna came home with a pizza from town, Milo was lying face down on the grass in a pool of blood.

The day of Milo's funeral I locked myself in this bathroom and cried until I threw up. I imagined Milo crinkling to the grass after the bullet went smashing through his temple. I imagined the bits of gray brain that wormed their way between the green blades. I imagined the dark black of his blood, the hose the medics used to wash it away. I imagined the way that his skin sunk to his bones moments later. I'd been at the house a few months before and Milo was obsessively playing pool against himself in the game room. His dark hair was unwashed and stuck to his forehead in serpentine clumps. He was small for his age, feminine-looking; long lashes and wide, open blue eyes.

"We'll show you how it's done," Nick told him, taking a cue down from the wall. But Milo shook his head. "I'm practicing," he said. "Alone." Every time we went to go outside, we could hear the clack of pool balls coming from that room. We ignored him. It seemed to be what he wanted.

But what made me cry wasn't really Milo. It was the hole Milo left that frightened me; it was a hole I suspected could never be filled, and one I felt edging closer. At this point, my mother had been sick with cancer for nearly five years. Her death was in every absence. It was in the quiet of the air when the phone didn't ring, in the emptiness of a white wall, in the sleeping moments of the cat. It hung around my hands and hair like a fog, getting thicker with every progression of the disease, with every failed drug.

The first year Nick and I dated, our freshman year of college, I lived in a dorm that used to be the women's infirmary, back when the women's college was separate from the men's. Each room still seemed like a hospital room, complete with a sink and cold slate floors. The building was u-shaped and when the winds picked up in winter, they'd shriek against the stone. I had fevers that year, fevers and hives for no reason anyone could detect. And Nick sat up with me boiling water in the electric kettle, making me powdered soups and tea. He joked about the ghosts of the dead girls and made weird hoo-ing sounds before I'd fall asleep, but in my fever dreams, they would appear, the dead girls, their cheeks sanguine, their eyes sad. They'd be dressed in plain cotton gowns and they would show me their hands, always too small for their bodies.

I put my hand on the porcelain sink beside me. It's solid and cool and real and I wish I could carry it out with me, sit it beside the table. I have to get back to the dinner. Nick isn't going to come and find me, though I wish he would. I wish he would come down the hall and knock on the door and make hoo-ing sounds.

Nick still hasn't touched his food, but the blond woman is busy talking with the two women next to her. She doesn't turn to face me as I slip back into my chair. I put my hand on Nick's leg under the table. He gives me a sideways glance.

"We haven't seen Becky in years," I can hear Gray saying.

"Becca," Anna says.

"What?"

"It's Becca, Gray." Gray shrugs and leans closer to the bearded man he's talking to. He sits on the opposite side of Anna and she leans away from Gray as he moves over her. "I think we've got a wedding in the future," he says conspiratorially. He's drunk. Nick breathes in sharply and grabs at the beer again. I take my hand back.

It's delicate and resilient at once, the tiny thread holding me here. After Milo's funeral, Gray collapsed in my lap on the sofa and sobbed. I love you, he kept repeating. Never stop telling your mother that, Becca. Never stop telling your family how much you love them. No one else was in the room and when I told Nick he was mortified.

After dinner, Gray suggests that we all go for a walk on the property. There's a trail that leads out near the pond, into the woods beyond, up a small ridge to a clearing. Nick and I spent many hours one summer with hoes and weed clippers, clearing that trail.

There's polite talking as the guests get on their coats. The blond woman isn't really dressed for a hike. She's got on red clogs and her coat is a long camel-colored suede. I wonder if she's new to these parts, if she came out here to forget. She's not doing a good job, if that's the case.

There are five guests. Two of the women have permed helmets of brown curls. One is tall and buxom, the other is short and slight; but they both wear boxy wool blazers and simple neutral pants with shoes that resemble brown bricks. And there's the bearded man with his angular wife who keeps nervously reaching out to touch him as though he might vanish. Nick grabs my puffy coat off the hook in the mudroom and tosses it to me. He shrugs himself into an old wool hunting jacket I've never seen before. He comes up beside me and smooths my hair back, yanks on a handful until I'm turned to face him, then he leans down and puts his nose against my jaw.

Everyone else is already outside. Their voices are getting less defined as they walk down the lawn to the start of the trail.

"Sorry about this," Nick says.

"About what?"

"About what," he says shaking his head. "Right."

I can choose. He might be sorry about bringing me here, into this wound of family that can't seem to heal. He might be sorry for Gray's drunkenness, for Anna's silence, for the blond woman's confession, for the fact that we'll have to spend the evening in the woods with five strangers. He might just be sorry. Sorry for leaving me when he did, sorry for returning with streamers of pain rustling behind him, sorry for my mother's descent, for the fact that once she's gone I will be without family. Sorry for the tilted world. Or simply sorry for himself.

We trail behind the group and Nick takes my hand as we pass the pond. How long did it take Gray and Anna before they could come out here again? Before they stopped seeing Milo on the grass, Milo against the sky, Milo in all the geese flying by? Or do they still see him, feel him in the night breeze, see his thin, gangly frame scurrying in the distance, playfully dodging them?

I move my thumb over Nick's thumb and feel a wash of tenderness.

The group has fallen silent. The wind blows through the boughs of the pine trees, rushes over the pond. Even the animals are quiet in the barn down the driveway.

There's a couple of benches by the pond, before the start of the trail, and Nick pulls me over to one. We sit close together. Behind us, the group continues to walk. Soon they'll be in darkness, the woods lit only by Gray's headlamp.

I didn't see her hang back.

"Can I sit?" Anna asks.

"Of course," I say, gesturing to the spot beside me.

She closes her coat around her and hunches into it, sinks to the bench. The group's footsteps disappear into the woods.

"How's your mother doing, Becca?" she asks. I have stock responses to this question, depending on who asks it. Status quo, not well, very bad. No one ever really wants to hear about it and so I try to keep the answers short. She's dying. I could say this. And it's not the graceful fade-out of death in the movies. They use knives and poisons but somehow she survives it. Though they cut off her breasts and scraped out her lymph nodes, though her diaphragm is paralyzed from radiation so that she can't breathe without tubes, though her arms fill with fluid making her fingers numb, though she's lost the hair on her face so that her eyes look like a frog's, somehow she makes it to the next round. Is this amazing or horrific, this desire to live? And at what point does the balance tip? At what point is she more dead than alive?

But she's still here. She still makes jokes about the dog and gets angry with the doctors. She can't figure out how to use her cell phone or get the stains out of the grout in the kitchen. But when I touch her skin, the heat is different. There's a defeat and a fury right below the coolness of it and it's a frightening combination—defeat that won't do you in and fury that can't save you. And sometimes I try to imagine the silence that will fall everywhere after she dies. I call her now with an offhanded question about taxes or recipes and I think that soon there will be no answers. And the question mark will lose its curve, will grow and straighten inside of my ribs, getting so large and sharp and unwieldy that it finally splits my body in two.

"She's hanging in there," I say. Anna nods. We don't look at each other.

"Give her my love," Anna says.

Only the whisper of wind through trees, only the distant throaty singing of frogs.

"Do you want to walk, Bec?" Nick's voice bangs against the air. Anna stands and takes a flashlight out of her jacket pocket. She twists the head of it until a dim nickel of light lands on the dirt.

"Come on," she says, gesturing with her head. "We should catch up."

Nick walks quickly, gets ahead of us, and then stops near the trees to wait.

There's something between Anna and me right now, something warm and desperate and sad. I want to ask her what she hears when Milo comes to her, when he materializes out of wind and light. Does he simply sit near her? Is it like she's pregnant with him again? Does he get lonely? Does he tell her why he did it? How the gun felt? What that moment was like when his finger tightened around the trigger? Did he think about Anna, the powdery smell of her neck, the drugged feeling of sleeping near her when he was small? Was it brilliant, that smash of pain? Did he see colors? Did he feel love and sorrow surge up in his throat and go soaring out of him? Was that what death was? No longer needing to contain these feelings in your body? When suddenly, all the splitting song inside you is you, you are vapor and scream, wail and firework, blue, red and salt and the darkening sky? You are—finally—no longer a container—you are the things that once were contained?

Anna tried to kill herself a month after it happened. She took sleeping pills and locked herself in the bedroom. She took too many, though, and just threw them up. "I want to go with him," she screamed at Gray, or so the story goes. She screamed this over and over until Gray loaded her into the truck, took her to the psych ward, and had her sedated.

Anna's flashlight is on but we walk through the woods mostly by instinct. The small circle of light shines uselessly on pieces of earth and rock. I reach out in the darkness and grasp Nick's arm. He squeezes my hand between his arm and chest.

When we get to the top of the ridge, I can see the group at the far corner. Gray has a thermos and is passing it to the bearded man. The two permed women stand close together. The blond is sitting alone on a rock overlooking the property. Her knees are drawn up to her chin.

Did the angular woman and bearded man have a child die, too? Were we all going to sit on top of this ridge and hum? Would the dead come floating off the tips of trees, would the girls come back in their cotton gowns, would their shrunken hands scratch at my face?

A buzzing begins in my head. I want to go tearing off down the path, across Maine, across this enormous country, back to that other ocean. But I just stand there, staring into the night, Nick's arm clamping my hand to his rib cage. Anna walks over to the blond woman and sits beside her. Their bodies are darker and more substantial than night and I can see Anna's pale hand settle on the woman's neck. The woman bends toward her.

Maybe it's not Milo's return that Anna's seeking. Maybe she only wants the world to stop spinning for a moment. Maybe she's chasing a still point when the questions can't get asked, when she can stop feeling that bang of lightning against her sternum, stop that horrible hum that persists whether she joins it or not.

At the end of the clearing, Gray laughs at something the bearded man says. Nick takes my hand in his and pulls me toward them.

L O S T
A N D
F O U N D

IN MEMORY, I CAN SEE MY FATHER STANDING THERE, HIS THICK steak of a body coated in the light of the television set, his mind reeling, his life a set of cards stamped in symbols known only to him.

But much more precedes this. You remember, don't you, the way that I found him, curled like a fetus, wrapped in a dirty sheet in the middle of the desert?

I was out walking the dog in the hot Arizona morning, tumbleweeds and cacti punctuating the barren landscape. I liked the emptiness of this particular road. No cars whooshed by, no other dog-walkers walked. I could wake up, put on my shorts and wander for miles without seeing anyone. My dog trotted dutifully beside me but he didn't like to walk. I was the one that liked spending my mornings out here with my old, tired dog, the sun on our shoulders, the dusty desert air in our ears.

The dog hadn't shown interest in chasing jackrabbits—or anything, for that matter—in a number of years. I held his leash loosely, looped over my thumb. The leash was just part of the ritual, not a means of establishing control. But the day it happened, the day we found him, the dog became bizarrely animated, tugging wildly and leading me off the gravel road, into the sand and sagebrush, whining and gulping. Surprised, I fumbled for control, lost it, and followed him partly out of curiosity, partly because my thumb had become painfully entangled in the leash.

We walked a short distance to a patch of scraggly desert brush and there he was, a full-grown man, naked and curled like a comma, lying beneath the paltry shade of a damaged cactus. His eyes were closed in blissful delirium, his fists balled like a child's. He was humming faintly, starving, near death, and there was a note attached to him on a decaying piece of twine.

This is your father, the note read. Do as you will.

"My father!" I exclaimed to the dog. The dog looked up at me, sad and patient, and tugged back in the direction of the car. I wrapped my father as best I could in the sheet and dragged him behind us.

At home, the dog slept fitfully, twitching and snorting on the rug near the door. I rubbed ointment into my father's burned skin as he slept on the sofa. In his delirium he cooed and reached for my face. The touch of his hand was like the leg of a large, dry insect.

For a while, I sat on a chair, watching my father sleep. His eyes were set far apart in his face like a lizard's. Deep lines stamped his sweaty brow. His skin was burned, but the color beneath the burn was pink, nothing like my own olive skin.

As he slept, I began to grow nervous. That unblinking desert sky had left no room for doubt; but here in my living room, dark clouds gathered. What does a person do with a found father? It's easy to lose a father. They get sick, they get old, they die, they abandon. But no one ever finds a father—or at least this sort of thing is infrequent. I had no books on the subject, no similarly situated friends to ask for advice.

Would I have to take care of him? Dress him in a blue uniform and send him up the street to the French Immersion School? Or would he awake with a profession? A lawyer, maybe. Maybe a dentist. It'd be nice, I thought, if he were very wealthy.

I grew anxious for something to do. I figured that while he slept I could run to the store to buy him something to drink. He seemed so parched and leathery, dried up like jerky in the hot desert sun. But what should I buy him? Seltzer? Beer? Juice? Milk? I couldn't decide. I bought every beverage in the beverage aisle. Apricot juice to zinfandel. After all, it's not every day you find your father.

When I returned to the house, there he was, sitting upright, rubbing his eyes. Blue blue eyes the color of cornflowers.

"Father?" I asked him, setting the bags down on the beat-up floor. He squinted at me, stretched his arms up in the air, extended his legs out in front of him so that his kneecaps popped.

"Excuse me," he said and tugged a blanket from the arm of the sofa. With it wrapped like a towel around him, he got up and found the bathroom.

I filled the kitchen with the beverage bottles. Lined them up on the counter by color. Wine and berry coolers. Orange and carrot juices. Coffee and soda. The shower ran for quite a while.

"Can you find something for me to wear?" he called from the bathroom. I paused, looked at the bottles sparkling in the light.

Under my bed, where I keep journals and old letters and sweaters that I never wear, I also keep the clothes that Duncan left tangled in the sheets of the bed. They were all I had left of Duncan, except for a slow moving sadness. I probably should have tossed them, but I liked the way that Duncan smelled; the clothes were more potpourri than memorabilia. Two pairs of hospital scrub pants, one T-shirt with a faded monkey on the front, a pair of argyle socks with a hole in the toe, and one pair of plaid boxer shorts. I gathered up the clothes and slipped them through a crack in the bathroom door.

He emerged fresh, head erect, dressed in the monkey shirt and scrubs.

"I feel like a new man," he said. "A new man indeed." I smiled at him, but he wasn't looking at me, and anyhow the smile felt fake and nervous, a potato-head smile.

"Would you like something to drink?" I asked politely, not wanting to get off on the wrong foot.

"Actually," he said, "I'd love to go to a café. I'd like to get out and about."

Out and about, I thought.

"Do you want company?" I asked. I imagined the two of us, wide-eyed, drinking coffee out of heavy white mugs and talking all morning. We would clarify what the past twenty-nine years—

"No," he said. "Don't you bother. I'm up for a solo tour."

The dog woke up from where he was sleeping in the corner of the room and looked at me with ancient, patient eyes.

"Alright," I said, trying to mask my hurt. "There's a lunch counter two blocks away." I drew him a map. He smiled and nodded. His dark, wet-looking eyelashes were the only softness to his square face. I caught myself trying to memorize them—the black fringe around his cornflower eyes. What if he never returned? Would I be able to explain what he looked like? He reached out for the map, gently tugged it from my hands, winked, and walked out the door.

It took a long time to adjust to him. We had to go shopping for new clothes, and because he had nothing, I had to buy him things. We had very different taste and this proved troublesome. "It's my money," I insisted when he wanted the silk American-flag boxer shorts. He made short, snippy exhalations and then, "I'll pay you back."

He got a job changing oil at the garage down the street. No one there seemed to care if he came from Arizona aristocracy or a hole in the center of the earth. No one asked questions and no one expected answers. He brought home his meager salary and I turned my office into a bedroom for him.

We didn't talk much, my father and I. At first, I didn't want to pry. Maybe I was afraid he'd leave if I asked difficult questions, or maybe I was just afraid of what I'd find out. Soon we settled into the rhythms of co-habitation and the questions I'd had at first dissolved into the tickings of daily life. He would leave for work in the early morning, before I woke. I would hear him rattling things in the refrigerator, clanking around in the silverware drawer. He'd return in the late afternoons when I would be try-ing to work in the kitchen. He'd plod around, car grease on his chin, leav-ing dark, oily footprints on my white tile floor. He'd pop open a can of warm beer then stomp back into the living room to watch television.

"Did you see this?" my father called from the sofa, where I imagined he was placing his filthy feet. I bought the sofa only months before I found him and already it was beyond repair, the black smudges as deep as the batting.

"What?" I called from my computer in the kitchen.

"This show," he cried. "It's so crazy! They just torture these people while they have to answer questions and if they can answer the question anyway—"

"I don't care," I called back. A tiny silence and then,

"No need to be rude."

"Who's being rude?" I asked.

"Well, I think you are," he said.

I tried to type louder.

"Maybe I should try to win at a game show," he yelled.

I stopped typing. The words on my screen wiggled for a second, then grew still.

"Did you hear me?" he asked.

"Yes," I called back. "Yes, I heard you but I'm trying to work."

"Well excuuuuuuse me," he called.

I took a deep breath. My father.

Duncan never knew his father. This attracted us to one another at first. I could sit in the big bowl of loss inside him and then he could sit in mine. I knew nothing about my father, though, and Duncan knew everything about his.

Duncan's father was a psychotherapist who kept avid journals about his life. "Today," the journals read, "I woke and walked Mercy (the dog) through the neighborhood, thinking about the baby asleep at home." Each day was recorded carefully, and each day revealed a boring pattern like the day before. Duncan read and re-read the journals. He was fixated on them. To me, they were proof of how boring most people's lives are. To Duncan, they were the pieces of the puzzle, the clues to his father's suicide.

The journals had a lot to do with why Duncan and I split up. I couldn't listen to him read them anymore. We tried to go on a trip to Northern California. I wanted to see the ocean, the way it would break on the cliffs and spatter up into the sky. Duncan wanted to sit on the cliffs and read his father's journals. "Today," he read, "after walking Mercy, I returned home to re-read my notes about patient 106."

"Don't you ever get bored with that?" I asked. Duncan jutted his chin and raised his eyebrows. "No. I'm sorry if I'm boring you."

"It's just that we've read this part already." My voice was inadvertently whiny.

"This is all I have left of him," Duncan said. "I think that should matter to you."

The waves crashed against the cliffs and sent foam up into the sky but it didn't seem magical, like the image in my mind. Just water spraying up from the ocean and then falling back onto the rocks.

The truth is, it didn't really matter to me. The journals, Duncan's feeling of abandonment, the way he cried when we fought—as if I was dying. He used to reach for me when I was angry, his tan skin glistening, his fingers pulling me toward him. He would hold on to me as if I were a buoy and I would feel a little bit claustrophobic. I loved him but I didn't really understand that sort of grief.

I never mourned the loss of my father. My mother didn't talk about him, and by the time I was old enough to confront her, she was dying. He was a mysterious smoke way out in the distance. A forest fire that happened before I was born. I had no clues, no puzzle pieces to spend my life putting together. Just a clean, sharp hole. Duncan did not have this clarity; he lived amidst a dark bloody thing full of roots and broken teeth.

Eventually, Duncan started spending a lot of time with a girl named Lucy whose parents had died in a car wreck when she was young. I felt Duncan drifting away, toward another buoy, and I couldn't stop him. I'm not even sure I wanted to stop him. I watched his eyes fill with distraction, muddy with small dishonesties that eventually became large ones. And then, one day, he was gone.

I often wondered what it would have been like if Duncan and I were still together the day I found my father. Would it have given us hope—hope that our lives would be full of such unexpected fortune? Would he have seethed with jealousy? Or would he have seen the impending gloom hanging low on the horizon? Duncan always had a knack for detecting encroaching misfortune. "The movie is going to be sold out," he'd announce in the car on a Friday night. And then, "I just had a feeling," he'd explain after we'd been sold out of the show. "I just get a feeling about this kind of stuff."

But even if Duncan could have detected something gloomy, what could I have done? You can't just leave your father to die in the desert after almost thirty years without him. Surely Duncan would have understood that.

It's conceivable that Duncan would have been jealous of me. My father had vanished from my life completely, leaving no trace, thereby leaving a vast potential for reappearance. Duncan's father had killed himself, his stiff body a cruel reminder that he would not be there later, to comfort, instruct, or console. Duncan's loss was permanent; mine, permeable. There is such a thing as love linked by the absence of a father.

And if the father reappears?

But it hardly mattered. Duncan vanished not because my father re-entered. The reason for his departure lay in the negative space of the things I didn't do, the kind of loss I didn't feel. Lucy's bowl of loss was shinier, more pregnant with possibility, her long fingers limber with need.

I made my father a set of keys for the house. Silver for the front door, gold for the back. He could never remember which key was which and so most days he would press the doorbell in a perky three-ring succession to get in.

"I made you keys," I would say as I opened the door.

"I know. But I just can't remember which one is which," he'd say breezily, giving me a half-cocked smile. Sometimes he'd leave the keys at home in the morning. I'd find them under a stack of newspapers or wadded up in an old lunch sack of his beneath the kitchen table.

"Sometime I might not be home when you lock yourself out," I chastised.

"Ohhhh, you're always home," he said, his hair greased in rigid little ropes over his thinning pate.

He was a very messy man, my father. He never learned any discipline when it came to tidying up after he used something. He'd leave the olive oil on the counter, bags of herbs strewn around it like windblown trash. His socks gathered in little heaps and his bedroom began to smell sweet and fetid. I'd be in the bathroom brushing my teeth and that strong, footy smell would come wafting through the door. Sometimes, when he went to work, I'd gather armfuls of his dirty laundry and throw it in the washer. I'd strip his filthy sheets, streaked with oil residue and dotted with toenails and hair, gather the damp towels, straighten the stacks of papers and magazines. When he came home, he'd either pretend not to notice, or he really didn't notice, that the room was orderly, aired out. This, more than the fact that I cleaned his bedroom in the first place, always infuriated me, causing me to bang pans around while cooking and to burn my hand on the oven rack.

And then my father began to bring home friends. Large, pomaded men from the garage suffering from various degrees of bowleggedness.

"Hey, it's the missus!" they'd cry when they stomped in, a parade of oily feet, oily fingers dragged against the white walls. They'd gather on my small back patio, smoke cigarettes and drink beer until the moon hung bright above them. I tried not to listen to them talk but words slipped through the screen, over the tiles and into the kitchen. Women, car payments, garage politics.

I purchased a pair of earplugs. Fancy ones made out of an expanding gelatin. I sat in my kitchen and worked and pretended they weren't there. But eventually more and more friends began to appear. My father is popular, I realized. Ten friends crammed on the back patio gave way to fifteen. Then twenty. Brothers and cousins of the bowlegged men spilled down the patio steps, into the small parking lot I shared with my neighbor.

"Look," I told him one night when he came in to go to the bathroom. "We have to discuss this." I gestured toward the mob of greasy heads bobbing outside the kitchen window. My father paused, furrowed one eyebrow.

"This isn't your personal ballroom," I told him. "You can't just invite the entire garage over every night."

"It's not every night," he said, wiping his brow with his forearm. "I have to go to the bathroom."

He began to walk away. I fingered a stack of papers with my thumb.

"No! Wait a minute. It's my bathroom, my house. You're staying here. You can't just do whatever you want whenever you want. There needs to be rules," I said.

He blinked incredulously at me.

"Rules?" he asked.

"Rules," I said.

"What kind of rules?" His blue eyes turned a shade darker.

"Rules," I said, "so that I can get something done around here. Not everyone in the world has your hours."

"I'm your father," he said gravely. "Watch how you talk to me."

"You may be my father," I said, "but you're making me crazy."

"Ah, well, family's like a tin of nuts—"

"No, really," I stated. "Really you can't just come in here and take over everything. I spend hours every morning bleaching oil stains off the walls. If this doesn't stop you're going to have to find somewhere else to live."

An awful silence ensued. He looked at me, then at the floor. He raised his dirt-lined hand to his hair and stood with one palm pressed against the back of his head.

"Are you threatening me?" he finally asked.

Again I thought of Duncan. Some people go chasing these phantoms all their lives. Each day begins with a shadow of loss that hangs with the curtains, each evening comes to a close with a list of ways things could have been. And here was my answer to all of that, standing puzzled and wounded in front of me.

"Maybe I am," I said to him. "I guess maybe I am."

He entered the bathroom.

I sat reading the same line over and over again.

What was I supposed to do? The men outside laughed big full laughs and a bottle of liquor fell and broke on the cement.

When my father came out of the bathroom, his cheeks hung sadly. "I'll tell them all to leave," he said and walked slowly out the door.

Soon all the men went back to wherever they came from and my father traipsed in, closing the door with a pathetic click. He gave me a hurt look as he wandered past me into the living room.

The next few days my father returned from work silently, sighing and shifting in boredom. He would examine the contents of the fridge, pick up each container and then set it back down. He'd get out a deck of cards, sit next to me and shuffle them. He brought home a book of word finds.

"Can't anyone else have people over?" I finally asked him. "Why don't some of your friends ever have parties?"

He shrugged. "Doesn't work like that," he muttered.

The morose mood that settled over him made him even more of a slob. Dirty Q-tips appeared behind the bathroom trash can. Beer cans wedged between the sofa cushions. And the smell that came from his bedroom grew danker and more difficult to air out. Each morning I wandered the house with a mug of coffee, picking up the residue of his depression, burning piñ   ion incense and scented candles. The house began to smell of a nauseating mix of foot, earth, and flower. The dog began to sleep with one paw draped over his snout, trying to create a little puddle of dog air to breathe. I began to get headaches.

And then the phone calls started. Every hour the phone would ring. Even during the hours my father was at work.

"Is your father around?" the voices would ask. Men, women, even small children called. I took messages for him in a spiral binder. First one filled, then another. At night, he would sit in his bedroom, the phone dragged in, and return phone calls until I went to sleep. Who did he talk to all those nights, hunched over in his pungent bedroom? I didn't ask and he didn't tell me.

The mood was tense and the air thick. The dog began to tremble in his sleep. I would hear his tags rattling from the kitchen and go to him, stroke his ears until I soothed him back to silence. But I couldn't soothe him for very long; he'd quickly begin again and soon the trembling occurred even in his waking hours. It interfered with his eating, he limped, and his joints quivered. Then one day, I let him out in the side yard for a minute while I was writing and when I went out to fetch him, he was gone.

Sometimes you lose something—an earring, a sweater—and you have a sharp hope that it will turn up, as if signs will point you back to the missing object. I walked every street of the neighborhood hollering for him. I hung bright yellow posters of his face on lampposts, on bulletin boards at the grocery, lunch counter and nearby church. I even prayed. But the loss felt final. Infinite.

"Look what you've done!" I said to my father, my voice breaking.

"I wasn't even home when it happened. I didn't do anything," he said.

"He couldn't deal with the stress between us."

"What are you talking about?"

"All the phone calls, the crap everywhere—"

"I think you're the one with the stress problem," he said, turning toward the fridge to grab a beer. "You need to chill out or you'll die young."

"Wouldn't that be a blessing," I said hotly, slamming out into the side yard to fume and miss my dog.

I went to the pound every Friday afternoon just in case he'd been brought there without his tags. I became friendly with the woman behind the counter.

"Sorry, Hon," she'd say when I opened the door, the bells on the handle dinging. "No beagles today." I would walk the strip of cages, looking at all the dogs, their dark, shining eyes pleading or distrustful. I'd walk slowly, lingering, allowing the plaintive barks to bounce off my tired body.

I was looking at my favorite little dog—a runt with a bad case of mange but a sweet, polite way of barking—when I felt this cool, highly charged, shadow of wind pass behind me. It felt like a ghost, or what I would imagine a ghost feels like, passing by you in a tunnel of barking dogs. I turned to see.

He looked older, his hair short and his body lanky. His shoulders stooped; I didn't remember this about him. I felt glued to the concrete.

"Duncan?" I said, walking towards him. He looked over. He seemed not to recognize me, a cloudiness over his face, and I imagined I was seeing things. But quickly his face broke into a grin.

"No way," he said. "No fucking way." His teeth were still crooked. They made him look honest.

We went out for coffee.

Duncan was always a beautiful boy, and he grew into a beautiful man. His skin shone like copper rocks in a river and his eyes had this feline watchfulness, green as those bright spots in the sea.

We drank coffee and talked of the three years that had passed since we had last spoken. He had moved with Lucy to Santa Fe. She had wanted to open a jewelry store, but the money got tight and the relationship fizzled and he moved back to Arizona.

"I wanted to call you," he said sheepishly. "But I was too ashamed." My heart soared and plunged; I felt a little sick. Duncan was peering at me from over his coffee cup, his eyes greener in the light of the window. I was trying not to look at him, taking store of the cars in the parking lot. Three red ones in a row, flanked by trucks. A nice, cosmic symmetry. And then, suddenly, he laughed.

"I'm sorry," he said. "Tell me about yourself, what you've been up to."

I looked at him.

"Well," I said, "for starters, I found my father." Duncan's hands were wrapped around his coffee mug, set on the lacquered table. I watched to see if he would move them but they remained still.

"What do you mean?" he asked gravely.

"Just that," I said. "I mean I found him."

"I thought he was dead."

"So did I."

A long silence.

"So he wasn't dead?" Duncan asked skeptically.

"Duncan, I really don't know."

Some internal debate was brewing inside him. Did he not believe me?

"Okay," he said decisively. "You found him. That's great! You know, you look good," he said, leaning back in his chair. "You look really happy. Your skin and your hair. That must it be it, right? Your father."

I tried to tell him the story, but he seemed pained, and besides, every detail felt like it needed to be edited. The explanation sounded vague.

"I'd love to meet him," Duncan said, leaning forward again, reaching across the table to take my hand. "I mean, if that would be okay with you."

I felt, in a way, that Duncan was testing me, that he didn't really believe what I was telling him. In Duncan's world, fathers died and stayed dead. They left their regrets hovering in the heat that the skin of the bereaved gives off, in the condensation of breath. They left boxes of journals—mean little mementos to remind the living of the futility of life.

"Well, he works a lot." I could see Duncan's eyes grow suspicious. "But I suppose we could work something out. If you really wanted to—I mean, if you think—"

"I want to," Duncan said. "I want to, really."

We traded phone numbers and I returned to my house, a crazy shaking in my arms that wouldn't stop.

I had wondered what Duncan would have thought if he'd been there when I found my father, his arm linked loosely through mine. But I had never considered what it would be like for the two of them to meet after my father was back in my life, as permanent as a hum in the pipes. I had never actually imagined my life with either one of them, let alone both. What would they say to one another—these men with claims to my past?

When Duncan left me, I didn't really miss him. In fact, I had sort of enjoyed the idea that he had earned my spite. That I had a free pass not to like him and could feel completely guiltless about it. My friends sympathized with me. They banded against him.

But there's something about seeing a lover after a long time without. The sharpness of the thing that came between us was difficult to recall. He had betrayed me. But then, hadn't I also betrayed him? There is betrayal in not relating to the person who has become a part of you. In setting yourself apart from the pain of your lover.

The house was empty when I returned. I had deadlines looming but couldn't settle down to work. I turned on the television in the living room. I turned on the radio in the kitchen. I turned on all the lights. I started the dishwasher. I cleaned out the fridge.

I was repotting every plant in the house when my father walked in. He was still sore at me for banning his parties.

A strange thing happened then. I looked at his face, really looked at it. His skin was a little puffy around his eyes, his stubble dark and thick. Lines had deepened further into his brow. Touchable, traceable lines that grew shallow and almost imperceptible before his receding hairline began. His eyes were a brilliant, pale blue, too shocking for his plain face. And his lips—his lips were so pink. It hurt my heart to look at them.

My father, I thought, incredulously. My father.

I stood up from where I was crouched over my African violet, soil wedged beneath my fingernails. There was suddenly so much I wanted to say to him. About living without him all my life, about finding him, about the obvious stress this put on our relationship, about his life before me, about my life before him—

Words raced, tried to arrange themselves into sentences.

My father went to the fridge and took out a beer. He unscrewed the cap, set it on top of the fridge, tipped his head back and took a long, deep swig. Slowly, looking straight into my eyes, he swallowed and let out a rolling burp. Without saying anything, he kicked off his oily shoes and plodded into the living room to watch television.

The feeling of tenderness vanished.

I squeezed my hands into fists, then flattened them against my thighs.

I still felt jumpy and wanted to tell someone about finding Duncan. I could hear my filmmaker friend in New York. "You found Duncan at the pound?" she'd ask. "You've gotta be kidding. I should come back to Arizona and do a project about your lost and found life."

I walked into the living room and stood behind the chair where my father was sitting, his ankles crossed, watching baseball bloopers. He pretended not to hear me come in.

How could I have Duncan meet my father if we couldn't clear up this tension? Waves of nervousness started in my stomach and I went back into the kitchen to make some peppermint tea.

I looked around. Along the baseboard, smudges of dark oil residue screamed my father's presence. The trash can was perpetually full to bursting. The beer took up an entire shelf of the fridge, forcing the bread onto the counter, the bottles of juice out into the laundry room. I had taken to buying potato chips and mayonnaise, things I had ruled out as a matter of ethics long ago. I set up a workstation beneath the kitchen window, since my father had taken over my office. So much had shifted in such a short time. I began to drum my fingers on the table. This helped me with my nerves. I was getting a real rhythm going when my father came in. He went to the fridge and began foraging for dinner. Leftover Chinese food, cheese, apple sauce.

I didn't know where to begin.

"Dad," I imagined saying. But I hadn't been calling him that. "Father," I would say. "Father, I have this friend I would like you to meet." How contrived. I couldn't say that. We didn't have that kind of thing going. I'd just have to bring Duncan over and hope for the best.

But I'd be paralyzed by the nervous larva wiggling in my stomach. I'd be sick with nerves.

My father was busy making some sort of Chinese food melt in the toaster oven. The smell reminded me of my missing dog.

"How was your day?" I asked. He turned his head in my direction.

"Who wants to know?" he asked.

"I do," I said.

"Fine," he said.

"Great," I said.

"Gross, there's rice in the silverware drawer," he said. "Yuck."

"I have an idea," I began, sarcastically. "You could clean—"

This wasn't going anywhere.

My father began to scratch his inner thigh. I began to drum my fingers again. This time, though, it didn't help. The phone rang. My father turned, his face lit up, and he trotted off to begin his night of talking to whomever it was he talked to.

There's no way in, I thought hopelessly. My father. How embarrassing. What would I tell Duncan? "I'm ashamed of him, Duncan. All of your life you've wanted a father and now I have mine and I don't want anyone to see him."

Suddenly, my father stalked back into the kitchen.

"Phone's for you." The receiver smelled faintly of beer breath.

"Hello?" I asked.

"Was that him?" Duncan asked in a gossipy, conspiratorial tone.

"Um. Yeah," I said.

"That's amazing."

"How's it going?" I asked.

"It's fine. Sorry to break the three-day etiquette thing, but I figured I knew you well enough to call when I wanted to."

"Oh. Yeah. Sure," I said. Who did Duncan think he was? The larva in my stomach started up again.

"So, I was thinking about having breakfast at the little lunch counter near your house on Saturday, I guess that's tomorrow, and I was thinking that would be a great time for us all to get together."

I looked over at my father who was standing, hypnotized, in front of the television. He had turned off all the lights and was bathed in different colors from the screen. It made him look a little spooky.

"Tomorrow?" I asked.

"Yeah, how does that sound?"

"Gosh, Duncan, I don't know how to say this but—"

"What?" Duncan asked.

"Well. I guess—Well. It's just that things have been a little topsy-turvy and. It's just—I'm not sure that. Well—"

"Don't overthink it," he said. "You guys just meet me at the counter at eleven. That's not too late right?"

"Eleven? I guess not, but—"

"See you then."

He hung up.

Now I was in a bind. I could show up alone and Duncan would think I had been lying; I could stand him up and it would seem like I had been lying; or I could bring my father and hope that he behaved, well, fatherly.

"Hey," I said to my father. "We have breakfast plans." He glanced over his shoulder at me.

"Says who?"

"Says my ex-boyfriend, Duncan."

"You had a boyfriend?" my father sneered.

"We're meeting at the lunch counter at eleven tomorrow. Okay?"

"Fine with me," he said, cracking his knuckles.

I stood there, watching the lines of my father's body. He was not a tall man but he had a sort of presence. His arms were thick with ropes of muscle. His neck was wide and short. His build didn't indicate a delicate spine—no gorgeously stacked vertebrae. Instead, he looked bolstered up by a large pole of metal.

I thought about the way that blood goes through the body. The liquid seems to know exactly which way to go, as if every cell in the body has a tiny, thoughtful brain. I thought of my father's blood, my father's bones, the ligaments that held him upright like that, his arms crossed, his legs apart.

How smart the body is. I closed my eyes and felt my own blood racing through the tubes of my veins, making my hands and feet warm. I wished I could ask those tiny brains what to do.

My father's Chinese food melt lay half eaten on a plate on the coffee table. Some noodles had fallen on the floor, glued there by orange cheese. He'd already gone through two beers, the bottles wedged haphazardly between the couch and the wall. His socks were off, as usual, and thrown like bait into the center of the room.

In that moment, my impatience with him ebbed. I'm not going to lie and say that I was filled with a strong, peaceful love. I just felt resigned. And this felt like progress.

"So eleven, then." I said. "I guess we'll just walk over there a little before, okay?"

My father didn't turn around. "Whatever you say. You're the boss around here."

The room flashed in reds and blues from the television. Strange shadows came and went.

"I guess I'm going to bed now," I said. "Goodnight."

"Mhmm," went my father and then guffawed at the commercial.

I went into my bedroom with a strange, heavy emptiness and lay in bed for a long time without sleeping. I would get up in the morning, I reasoned, clean the house, get dressed, have coffee so I was alert before the lunch counter encounter, and then we'd head over there together.

Somewhere, in between thoughts, I fell asleep.

In the morning, I woke up exhausted, a feeling of failure in my bones— dream residue. I looked at the clock. Ten-thirty. "Shit," I said, throwing myself out of bed. "Fuck fuck fuck." I threw on a robe and dashed into the bathroom. I began to strip off my pajamas when I realized that the bathroom was spotless. The sink wiped clean, the toilet seat down. The razor and shaving cream that usually crowed my toothbrush jar off the shelf above the sink were gone. I put my robe back on and went out into the house to find my father.

Each room was completely clean.

The door to my father's bedroom was shut. I knocked.

"Father?" I called. And then, "Dad?"

I cracked open the door. The room was spotless. My father's Tupperware storage containers of clothes and shoes were gone. The notebooks of his phone messages, also gone. The only thing that remained was the futon, sheetless, and the empty bookshelf.

I went back into the living room and sat on the couch. At that moment, all I could think about was Duncan, waiting expectantly for me at the lunch counter, and me sitting there with no father to prove myself by. I imagined Duncan's face—all sympathy at first, hardening into distrust.

"He's gone," I'd say. "I woke up this morning and he was gone as suddenly as he came, like a dream father." Duncan would tilt his head back knowingly, his eyes looking down his long, perfect nose. "But," I'd say, "it wasn't a dream."

The stillness of the house clung to my skin, sticky and disconcerting. The feeling in my stomach was dark and heavy, a slick precipice of granite rising. One last larva wriggled and grew still.

I would surely blow it with Duncan now—there was no doubt about it. He'd excuse himself and tell all of his friends how I had lost it since the breakup.

I began to work myself into a panic about it, searching the house for details that would prove that I had had a father. He couldn't just come into my life, turn my house on its head, and then vanish without a trace. There had to be a note, a photograph, something.

My head began to pound. I was frantically turning the sofa cushions over, looking for beer bottles and petrified cheese when I heard it—a soft whimpering coming from the side door. For a moment, I couldn't move. And then I walked over and placed my head against the cool whiteness of the door.

REALISM

SYLVIE IS TRYING TO SLEEP IN THE DARKNESS HIS SHADOW CASTS BUT it's difficult to sleep in the same room as a monster. When her father died he told her to be careful. These were the only words he left her, like leaving a bar of soap in a dirty handkerchief: What was she supposed to do with it? The monster had come the night before; he was terrible and scaly and had these long toothy fangs. But he was a sad monster, crying and lonesome, so she decided not to call anyone—the exterminator or anyone—but instead to sleep beneath his watchful gaze, his large tears splashing over her face.

2.

The next day at work Sylvie has difficulty concentrating. She screws up the cash register twice and tips over the jar of knives, cutting her knee. She has deep half-moons stamped beneath her eyes. She's tired; it's difficult to sleep. She wants to tell her friend Janice but can't think of a way to get from one end of it to the other.

3.

From work she doesn't go home. She goes straight to her mother's house. She wants help with the monster but her mother's in one of her funks. She's been digging large holes in the yard, putting the soil in shopping bags and bringing it inside the house because, as she tells Sylvie, the neighbors were trying to steal it.

4.

Sylvie returns home hoping that the monster will have gone but there he is, eager to see her, holding a plate of salad he's made for her. His eyes are dark brown and alive with hope. She feels a softness in her chest and wants to run but also wants to feel each bone of his snakeskin toes.

5.

Outside, on the way to work again, the cars seem like little boxes of normalcy, like toys sent from God. She wishes that the roof would lift off of her house and that the sun would flood every corner with light.

6.

She tells Janice that there is a monster in her house. Janice laughs and asks if she's talking about Andy, and Sylvie shakes her head and says, no, a real monster. Janice's eyebrows furrow. She says, Sylvie what are you talking about? and Sylvie describes him—tall as the light fixtures and full of muscle —scaly, dark browns and grays. Janice shakes her head and says that she has to go do inventory.

7.

The monster slowly begins to shrink and Sylvie realizes that this is what will happen. He is like one of those capsules that turns into a sponge except he is the other way around; when he is a capsule she will just throw him out.

8.

What shocks Sylvie is that the next time she goes to visit her mother, her mother is also shrinking. When Sylvie asks what is happening, her mother's eyes grow wide and tears form and she says that she is dying. Sylvie doesn't know whether to believe her. She follows the mother down the hallway and the mother takes out a bag of gold rings. These are for you, she sobs, all the family heirlooms.

9.

Gradually both the mother and the monster shrink down to miniature form. The monster in miniature is very cute, like a little playmate, harmless and wet-eyed and full of laughter. The mother, on the other hand, is very disturbing. Sylvie brings her to the hospital in a cat box and the doctor examines her, shrugs his shoulders and pronounces that she is growing smaller.

10.

Sylvie quits her job; it is just too difficult to concentrate and she burned a large pink scar into her thumb from the milk steamer.

11.

Eventually her mother moves in with her and meets the tiny monster. At this point they are both the size of mice. The mother and monster have such fun together. Sylvie realizes that her mother is much happier as a small person and also much more forgiving.

12.

The mother and the monster are slightly smaller than mice when they stop shrinking. This is also the size they are when they fall in love.

13.

Sylvie tries to tell her friends what has happened but her friends don't believe her. They say it's all happening in her mind and when she invites them over to see the mother and the monster, spinning happily across the linoleum in a waltz of small happy feet, the mother and monster hide so that Sylvie looks like a fool.

14.

Her friends chastise her for confusing her dreams with reality. It's not a dream, Sylvie insists.

15.

Sylvie rarely leaves her bedroom. The mother and the monster live unseen in their tiny delirium until they are old and frail. Eventually they die and their bones decompose quickly, leaving small heaps of bone dust on the kitchen floor. Sylvie also grows old but it's a lonelier version. She draws pictures of her late mother and monster to send to her friends but can never quite capture them—the jerky movements of their waltz, the round nubs of their chins, the way the light shone out of them when they were near each other, until she couldn't escape the heat in the house, though she sat in the darkness of her bedroom, a pan of ice by her head. How do you draw heat? she wonders. How do you draw a mother? A monster? How do you even explain it?

CELIA's FISH

THE GOLDFISH CELIA CHOOSES SEEMS TO LEAP INTO THE LITTLE green net, then into the bag from the net. Gerard wonders if it has some sort of mental problem. The fish is fat, fatter than its counterparts, and there's something mean and angular about its face. All the other fish look blank.

"Here you go," the kid with the net says; he snaps the rubber band around the top of the bag and hands it to Celia. The kid has rubbery skin. When he talks, it sounds like his tongue's engorged. His r's don't come out. Celia is eight. She holds the bag tenderly and delivers it to the counter. Gerard follows his daughter, extracting some change from his pocket.

Mandy's Pet Oasis is in the back of a drugstore, located next to racks of cheap flip-flops and vinyl sneakers. It's been here for years, though before today, Gerard had never been inside. Most of the lighting comes from the fish tanks along one wall, giving the whole store a gloomy, cinematic feel. Behind shelves of dog bowls, cat litter, and plastic fish castles, a few world-weary puppies stare through the wire of their pens. According to the laminated signs tacked above them, they're twenty percent off.

"You got a tank?" the kid asks. " 'Cause we got it on special today. Tank, filter, pebbles, food, castle, treasure chest, and pH stuff. All together." Gerard notices a little knob of silver glints from the kid's mouth. The kid gestures to a tank on a card table, filled with colorful plastic castles and reeds, wrapped in cellophane.

"We have a bowl," Gerard says. It's not true, exactly, but Marsha said she'd bring one over later. The fish is a dollar. It glares at Celia from the bag, but she's examining kitty collars on a wire tree next to the register.

"You got your fish?" Gerard asks her. She nods and drags the bag off the counter religiously, as though it's full of golden powder.

Gerard watches his daughter as she walks out of the store. She's been dressing herself lately. Today it's grape-colored shorts that have gotten too tight and a wrinkled, pink shirt. She's a strange girl, pale and brooding. And lately she's taken to walking crookedly, touching her shoulder to a wall, bouncing off it, then finding the next available surface to touch. She's got her mother Ellie's hair—or at least what Ellie's hair used to be—white blond, fine. It hangs straight down her back, ending in wispy curls that dissolve in the air.

"Hang a left, Celia-bean," he says. She's gotten distracted by a display of beach balls. She doesn't look at him, touches her shoulder to the display, and then heads diagonally out of the small complex of stores, cradling the little baggie in the crook of her elbow.

Gerard watches Celia navigate the sparse parking lot. She touches her shoulder to each car as she walks towards their blue Honda. Gerard unlocks the passenger door and Celia slides in with a grimace. The car is hot, airless, and it hurts Gerard's legs to sit on the vinyl. He rolls down his window but there's no breeze. He glances at the fish on Celia's lap. It's still glaring, this time at his leg. And as he turns the key, he imagines someone has planted a car bomb beneath them, the entire car will burst into flames and they will explode with it, body parts flying, hair burning, fish turning into a demon bird and fluttering off into the sky.

It's a short drive up to the hills where they live, and Gerard doesn't feel like talking. Marsha mentioned once that it was easier to have difficult conversations in the car—you couldn't see the other person's face—and sometimes when he's driving Celia around he thinks he should say something to her. I know how hard this must be for you. I don't know what to say to make this better. We're a team, you and me, and we'll get through it.

All the words sound stupid in his head and he can't bear to say the things he doesn't mean. Maybe somewhere in that eight-year-old mind she understands the whole situation better than he does.

Gerard pulls into the garage and Celia bolts out of the car.

"I'm showing Mommy the fish," she announces, and with her side crammed against the railing, she runs, leaning into the wall so that it looks like she's being lifted up the steps by a magnetic force. When Gerard follows, only minutes later, he finds Celia in his bedroom, stuck by the dresser. Ellie looks terrible; she's been crying and her face is blotchy through the sweat and grayish sheen. Her eyes are too wide. Vomit is cooling in the pan they keep near the bed.

"Hey, baby," she says to Celia, her voice quivering. "It's okay, you can come in." Ellie tries to smile but her lips look stretched and tight. She gestures to Celia. Then she convulses into a round of violent dry heaves. Celia inches toward the dresser, the baggie dangling.

Ellie's head scarf is crooked, and as she's heaving, it falls into the pan. Gerard puts his hand on Celia's back and maneuvers her out of the room.

"It's going to be okay, sweetheart," he says to her, crouching down to smooth her hair out of her face. She doesn't look upset. The look in her dark eyes isn't childlike, but jaded and distrustful. Celia jerks her shoulders and edges away from him. She's holding the bag so tightly it looks like it's going to pop.

"Let's put the fish in the kitchen. We'll acclimate him." Gerard stands, puts a hand on the thin bone of her shoulder and steers her down the hall. The fish's head looks large—it's the way she's squeezing the bag. He pulls a Tupperware out of the drawer and fills it with tap water, holds it out to her. She sets the baggie in it.

"This way he won't be shocked when we put him in new water," Gerard says. Celia chews on the inside of her cheek and watches the baggie float. "Can you entertain yourself for a bit, Bean? I'm going to go help Mommy." Celia shrugs. What's with her shrugging lately? Every question seems to get one.

"I'm traumatizing her," Ellie says when he comes back in the room. Tissues are wadded everywhere, collecting in the spaces between pillows. He takes the pan away and goes into their bathroom to wash it out. The counter is littered with orange bottles. There's an amazing variety; he has no idea how Ellie keeps track of them. She better keep her acuity for a while longer because there's no way he'll remember the order, the right amount of pain medicine, steroids, blood cell enhancers, anti-inflammatories, anxiety pills, anti-depressants, sleeping pills… Jesus. He wets a washcloth and goes out to sit next to her. He puts his hand on her greasy hair and strokes it as she stares dumbly at the wall.

This round she's been able to keep her hair. One of the drugs a few months back made it fall out and it grew back grayish and curly. Sometimes he looks at her, her hair in corkscrews, short, wiry and uneven (it never quite came back at her crown), her face puffy and pale, her skin starting to hang off her body—though she's only thirty-six, too young for this sort of age, and he doesn't recognize her. She's a reminder of Ellie, like someone with the same manner in a crowded restaurant.

It's hard not to imagine her dead—even now, running his fingers along her warm scalp, her rib cage expanding with her breath, her face damp, her fingers pressing into his leg—he feels her growing stiff. Sometimes at night he wakes up certain that the time has come—that she's stopped breathing—and there's something amazing about it—the way he rises out of himself, riding a tide of awe—and fear, too, but mostly awe. He feels relief when he puts his hands on her hot face but also dreads that this will continue on and on, that he will wake up every night of his life thinking about death—and the selfishness of this thought dissolves the dread into shame—

"Oh," Ellie says. She lays her head back against the pillow. "Oh. Fuck. The twisting again."

"Can I get you anything?" Gerard says.

"No," Ellie says. "I think I just need to rest."

Ellie decorated the living room when they moved into this house. Gerard settles into the cushions of the velvet sofa and stares at the abstract painting above the mantle. It was an odd choice for Ellie—dark colors, huge strokes of black and olive, some orange peeking out from behind darker spaces, pink and lavender gracing the edges like ethereal balloons. It's a brooding piece, but the rest of the room is warm, cluttered with Ellie's grandmother's basket collection and two old rocking horses, piles of blankets, pillows, magazines. Everything in this house is Ellie's; Gerard never cared for decorating. And when she's gone, Gerard imagines that all these objects will cry out for her, like dogs abandoned in a field. He'll have to get rid of everything—right down to the royal blue duvet that she bought him one winter when he complained the old comforter was too small. And then what will he do? Move himself and Celia to the backyard? Spend a year in a tent?

There's a knock at the door and the sound rescues Gerard from what would surely have become a stupor on the sofa. He goes over, turns the lock.

"Hi dear," Marsha says, leaning over to kiss his cheek. She smells strongly of coconut and the blood rushes to his head. She's wearing her gardening clothes—dirty jeans and a white tank top. Her red bra straps are bright against her freckled shoulders. She's carrying a wide-lipped fish bowl—it's not what Gerard expected. It's low and large and looks like someone sat on it while the glass was cooling. It's full of peaches.

"I stopped by the farmer's market on my way," she says. She walks past him. Celia appears in the hallway.

"Celia, baby!" Marsha says theatrically. She stops, props the bowl on her hip. A bit of her side shows where the tank top lifts. "How are things?"

"Okay," Celia says, shifting her weight to one foot. She's got a pad of paper in her hand and an empty backpack on; it's unzipped and the flap hangs down her back. "I'm kind of busy, though."

"Well, don't let me interfere," Marsha says and winks.

Celia disappears into her bedroom, closing the door. Gerard follows Marsha into the kitchen.

"That fish is ugly," she says, peering at the baggie. She runs water over the peaches.

"Celia chose it," he says. Marsha shakes her head.

"How's Ellie?" she asks. Her short hair is glossy and mussed. She's growing it out, she claims, and so she keeps the sides pinned up in funny little barrettes. Today they're all blue.

"She's having a bad day," Gerard says. He walks up behind her, too close; he can feel the warmth of her body through her clothes. The coconut is mixed with another smell, something warm and magnetic, almost spicy. He presses his nose against the side of her head. She keeps rinsing the peaches, but he can feel the tension shooting through her body. He's encouraged and puts his hand on her ass, slides it down between her legs.

"Should we bring some of these in for her?" Marsha asks. "We could cut them and put a little yogurt in a dish." She reaches up to the shelf next to the sink for one of Ellie's handmade bowls, and as she does this, he can't resist, he slips his hand under her shirt and turns her around to face him. She leans away and looks at him with that familiar danger in her eyes, coy and a little cold. He kisses her, open-mouthed and sloppy; she runs her fingertips down his chest.

"Not right now," she whispers and he untangles himself. She turns back around and opens the silverware drawer.

"Hey sugar," Marsha says, sitting on the side of the bed.

"Hi Marsh." Ellie says wearily. She's still propped on the pillows but it's clear she's been dozing. The room smells sharply of bile and old sweat.

"What did you bring me?" Ellie asks. She raises her hands to her hair and smooths it with an expert caress; it's a gesture left over from the old Ellie, the pretty, vain Ellie with a long mane of shockingly blonde ringlets. On the new Ellie it looks wrong, a grotesque impersonation. She pulls the cover up to her armpits and holds it there.

"I stopped at the market," Marsha says. "You wouldn't believe who I saw with Dale Kerchaw, that pig." Marsha sets the yogurt and peaches on the nightstand and straightens the stack of magazines. Ellie's face lights up. "That twenty-two-year-old nurse!"

Gerard backs out of the room to let them gossip. He knocks softly on Celia's door.

"Come in," she calls. She's sitting on the floor with eight dolls lined up in front of her. They're all on folded blankets or towels and none of them have any clothes on.

"What're you up to?" Gerard asks.

"I'm playing," she says. In her hands she's got a ballpoint pen and she looks a little guilty. He walks toward her and kneels.

"What are you playing?"

"Hospital," she says. "They're sick." And then Gerard sees that a bunch of the dolls have little holes in their arms, pressed into the plastic or cloth with the pen. The holes are small, black with ink around the edges.

"Why are you sticking them?" he asks, pressing his hands against a creepy looking brunette, its blue eyes trained at the ceiling.

"I'm helping them," she says.

Gerard waits. He's sure he will start to feel something. He looks at his daughter. Her dark eyes seem misplaced in her pale face. She has almost no lashes, no eyebrows, and yet she has his eyes, dark and large, and his over-sized lips. She's not pretty, though it's not clear why. All her features are handsome but they're poorly combined. There's something fishlike about her, actually.

"Isn't there another game you could play?" Gerard asks. Celia looks at him gravely and shrugs.

Why is it that no one around here can get enough of death? Even Marsha comes up to see Ellie almost every day. And though it's terribly kind, gives Ellie something to look forward to and gives Gerard a chance for carnal release—he can't help but wonder sometimes if she's a little bit attracted to the spectacle of decline. In some ways, it's more excruciating and exhilarating than any carnival ride or horror film. It's happening right in front of them, what they all fear most.

Gerard stands up.

"Maybe we should go put the fish in the bowl Marsha brought."

"Can you just do it?" Celia asks, twirling her pen. "I don't want to."

Outside her window, he can see the sun reflecting off Marsha's red car. They'd had sex in that car on Thursday. They'd driven out to look at the flower farms, to pick Ellie daisies and irises, and had parked on the side of a dirt road afterward, the flowers wrapped in paper, flung all over the back seat. Marsha leaned over the emergency brake and unbuttoned his pants. He was already hard when she ran her tongue down him, wedged her fingers below his balls. And then, as if they were still sixteen, she crawled over him, lifted her long, flowery skirt, slid her underwear off until it hung from one knee, and jerkily fit him inside her.

She came so easily. It was nothing like Ellie. He had to work for Ellie's pleasure. He had to go down on her, play with her, watch her arch and tense and then lose her focus, bring her back to center, keep the rhythm going. This is how it used to be, anyway. He hadn't had sex with Ellie in almost a year. They'd tried a few times but it was so depressing. She couldn't get into it, all the smells were off, and it ended in tears. Marsha did this thing with her hips and ass, pressing herself away from him a little, jerking angrily, and then she just came, loudly, unexpectedly, expelling air and noise like a sea mammal, her small eyes glittery and distant.

Gerard shoves his hands in his pockets. Celia is waiting for him to leave. He bites his bottom lip and feels a worm of longing roll inside him.

Celia looks down at her dolls, her posture full of purpose, and punctures another one with her pen.

Gerard rinses out the bowl and fills it with the water from the Tupperware. He takes the baggie and undoes the rubber band. The fish isn't looking at him. The fish is darting back and forth in the bag like it's looking for a corner.

One of these days, Ellie's going to slip into a coma. That's how it happens. Or for some reason, that's what Gerard has decided. One day, he's going to walk into the bedroom with a cup of tea and she's going to be staring glassily at the ceiling, just like that doll. He'll sit calmly on the bed with her, repeating her name. And then he'll call Marsha and the two of them will call the ambulance together—they'll watch as Ellie's loaded in, wrapped in her favorite afghan, the one her great-grandmother knit in stripes of avocado and red—and the doctors will admit her so she can have the right doses of things—or so she can have an IV bag, at least. And he and Marsha will sit vigilantly in a small, medicinal room, breathing in molecules of bodies on their way to becoming dust—and they will look at each other, he and Marsha, and sometimes they'll go back to her tiny house and eat cottage cheese with salsa and fuck in her cramped bedroom, both of them nauseous with lack of sleep, and people will probably send flowers, Ellie's obese sister Petra will probably show up, bearing some awful food for him, sausage lasagna or beef stew. And Celia will be home with a sitter. And sometimes he will bring Celia to the hospital. And that's how the end will be.

There's moisture around the top of the bag and Gerard moves his thumb and forefinger together so that they slide pleasurably, the two plastic sheets in between rubbing over themselves. The light through the window is clear through the murky water in the bag, and the fish shines. Does the fish know it's about to begin a lifelong incarceration? That it will swim in circles every day of its life? Or does the fish just exist for the moment—and what would that be like—to live every moment with no concept of past or future? If he could exist only in this moment, then he'd see only the fish and the water and the dirt particles and the light. He would feel that he tied his left sneaker too tight and that it's cutting off some circulation in his foot. He wouldn't think of Ellie's ravaged body—the smell of decay when you got close to her—sweet and fishy. He wouldn't remember what it was like before she got sick. How they used to collapse next to each other on the sofa after work and complain. God! What had they complained about? And he really did like the challenge of Ellie's body then—the way he had to work to bring her over the edge, to distract her from the stress of her mind, and then when he finally did, she shook and would hold on to him afterward, her long fingers kneading his while she dozed.

And then—shit! He's still holding the bag, but only one side of it, and there's water all over the floor, cascading off the counter, running down toward his feet. The fish is on the counter, flopping toward the edge in small, spastic jerks. He reaches for the tail, but it slips through his fingers. Dammit! He tries again. The fish is slick, muscular. It can't die. No! Not in this house, nothing else is going to die—cursed fish! It's cold and orange and has no pigment on one side, that's why Celia liked it. The feel of the fish between his fingers feels like something internal—something he has no right to be touching—and his insides get hot and his joints feel shaky but he pinches down hard and moves fast and manages to get the fish back in the stupid bowl.

"Fuck you," Gerard says to it. And then he turns to see if anyone has seen him. But he's alone in the kitchen, the bright blue wall, the white shelves, the glass jars full of herbs turning gray in the sun.

Gerard feels himself start to tremble a little and a pain starts shooting from his back into his head. His heart pounds furiously. He's dizzy. The room is getting brighter, slowly brighter—but not that slowly. The edges of the counter are getting so bright they're fading out. He's not okay. He's going to collapse. He's going to die and die first! He's sweating now, and this takes all his strength. He has to sit. His knees give gently, it's as though large hands are pushing him down, and then he's on all fours. He's spinning, an axe is banging on the bone of his forehead from the inside and something is too hot inside him. He can't breathe and his heart is pounding and his saliva is doing something weird—he can taste his saliva. As soon as he can stand up again, as soon as he stops tasting this—so bitter, like a plant he shouldn't be chewing on—as soon as he can breathe again he'll knock that fish onto the floor and he will be able to breathe because something will be let go, the soul of the fish will be let go. Gerard is sweating, a bead of it falls onto the parquet floor, his hand is turning white from pressing it down his body is spinning and spinning and there is Celia and Celia is talking to him and Celia is running toward the bedroom—

And he should take the fish outside because it's soul might get caught against the ceiling and hover and maybe he should make Ellie die outside too because her soul might get trapped in the house and then they would have to move but how could they sell the house to someone knowing Ellie's soul was caught in it? He's trying to get himself outside, scooting on his arms, trying to get toward the front parlor so he can die outside—they are all going to die outside, this is the only thing that makes any sense! This makes Sense! Ha! He's going to die first! And then there are hands on his back, grabbing him by the waist of his pants. What on earth, Marsha is saying, Gerard get a hold of yourself but he can't breathe—he's laughing! And there is Ellie, teary and odd-looking, holding on to the wall. He can see right through her! Ha ha ha ha ha ha ha! HA! He is going to die first and that will be something! Something no one could have expected!

It's the Xanax that Marsha gets from Ellie's stash that finally calms him. Marsha sets him up in the living room and turns on cartoons—a cat racing through a well-manicured forest. He feels so light. He feels so good, actually. Like his thoughts have been bleached and fluffed.

"Come sit with me," he says. Ellie's gone back to the bedroom. Marsha squints at him.

"I don't think that's such a good idea," she says.

"Just come here," he says, patting the cushion.

Marsha reluctantly sets her bag down and comes toward him. When she sits, she's stiff, her legs bent at ninety-degree angles, her feet parallel. Gerard wants to laugh. She looks like a diagram!

He turns toward her and puts his face against her chest. She stiffens even more, puts her hand on his head and pushes it away.

"Not now," she says. "Gerard, get a grip."

He leans away from her. Her face puckers, her eyes scrunch. And then Marsha starts to cry.

"Marsha," he says, reaching out for her shoulders.

"What the hell," Marsha hisses, slapping his hands away. "What are you doing? What was all that?" She stands. He can hear the rattle of her keys as she stalks down the hall. The front door opens and slams.

He would have chased her but he's fuzzy and warm and his thoughts aren't coming like they normally do. His thoughts are round.

The clatter of pans wakes him. It's dark out now. Dread hits him as soon as he's conscious, before he even remembers what happened. He stands and his knees crack. They're sore. He must have banged them on the way down.

Ellie's in the kitchen. She's dressed in her nice clothes—her red silk pants and an orange cashmere sweater; he hasn't seen these clothes in so long. They went to an opera once—Celia was smaller then, maybe six—and Ellie wore that sweater. Her hair is damp from a shower. She turns to look at him and her face is so serious, her pale eyes circles of concern.

Gerard looks at the wall clock. It's ten-thirty at night. Shit, he didn't make Celia dinner and now she must be asleep.

Ellie has a large pot on the stove.

"What are you doing?" he asks. She's put on makeup and you can't tell she's dying—not really. The eye shadow glimmers up to her eyebrow.

"I'm making soup. We didn't have a lot of stuff, but there were dried lentils and that beef shank in the freezer. And Marsha brought all those carrots."

Ellie hasn't cooked in two months, not since the pain got so bad she had to take pills on top of the pain patch. She barely has the energy to get back and forth from the bedroom to the living room to watch an hour of television. He stands next to her. She's wearing perfume, leathery and woodsy. The carrots are cut into small circles; the lentils are boiling, filling the room with their bean smell.

He looks at the fish. It's swimming in circles, flipping its body around and around. He takes the yellow container of fish food Marsha brought and shakes some into the water. The fish darts up and sucks the flakes down greedily.

Ellie sets down the knife and holds out her arms to him. Beneath the orange cashmere those arms are so thin, bruised from various injections.

"I'm so sorry, sweetheart," she says. She's crying. Soon they'll all cry so much they'll flood the house; they'll damage the foundation. She's shaking her head. The mascara leaves speckled tracks down her cheeks. He glances at the fish. It sucks down its last flake of food, stares blankly at its own reflection.

He walks over to her, takes her body. Ellie, he wants to say—just her name. But the room is silent. He's gripping her too tightly; he can feel her tensing away. But it's all he can do. He can't let go.

$\overset{A}{R} O M A N C E$

MRS. CAPP DIDN'T TELL ME WE WERE HAVING COMPANY THIS morning, but when the bell rings, she flies to the door as if she's been waiting all her life. The man's a bit of a hippie with long, wavy blond hair and an unkempt beard.

"Liza, this is Satan." She says his name with such assurance I can't be sure I've heard her correctly. She articulated the "Sate" part far better than the "An" part—and given his looks, he might be named "Seitan" or "Seat-Man" or "Slaton."

"Satan, like S-A-T-A-N?" I ask. He nods. I nod back. Mrs. Capp nods. Am I missing something? Mrs. Capp did tell me a few days ago that she met a man while browsing through the record store downtown. "Nice looking," she said. "And very knowledgeable about percussive jazz." She mentioned she might have him over sometime. But she didn't warn me that he was coming this Sunday morning.

"Nice to meet you," I say. I'm still in my pajamas reading the newspaper. In large, gothic font across the top of the front section are the words FIFTEEN DEAD IN NATIONAL TRAGEDY. Satan jams a thumb through the hammer loop of his painter's pants. He looks at the paper and I think I see his blue eyes twinkle, then he looks away guiltily.

A few months ago, Mrs. Capp placed an ad in the local paper looking for "a quiet and respectful female roommate with a low tolerance for untidiness and a high regard for manners." We didn't hit it off so well the day I met with her about the room, but since she didn't get many responses, I ended up moving in.

In the time that I've lived here I've gone on one date, a blind date engineered by my sister, Kate. Phil was very nice in a helpless kind of way. Kate knew him from college. He had thin blond hair and watery eyes that sat too far apart. After speaking each sentence, he'd pause as if his words needed time to percolate through a fine sieve. But most of the things he said to me were easy to digest, like, "I was born in Seattle." This sort of phrase wouldn't be in response to a question (such as "Where were you born?") but would serve as an awkward opener. I felt like I was supposed to do something special with Phil's silences; they seemed coded and livelier than his speech. Though I was curious about his manner, I didn't want to date him.

Mrs. Capp, however, has been out numerous times with numerous men—some of them quite young. One I recognized from my graduate program—a squinty young man, Kirk Williams. In class it seemed he was trying to see the projected lecture notes with his front teeth. I can't figure out where she meets these men because she doesn't go out much and when she does she wears unflattering pleated skirts and necklaces that hang down, accentuating a tired-looking bosom. I suspect she's one of those librarian types that men fantasize about. They seem maternal and prim, but get them in a dark room and va-voom, the buttons are flying.

Mrs. Capp was married once to a man named Sal. She's in her midforties now, a little overweight. Sal, I gather, was considerably older. He was a professor at the small school where she earned her master's degree. Two years ago he died of a stroke. Mrs. Capp speaks of him highly. She sighs at good meals and comments on how he would have loved the lamb, the potatoes, the flavor of the dry wine.

I get the sense, however, that she didn't really know him that well. The stories she tells don't seem specific. When I tell her about Thomas, my ex-boyfriend, I never say, "Oh, Thomas loved comedy films." Instead, I say that when he was a baby he was born with two thumbs on each hand. The doctors immediately cut off the extras and Thomas was still sore that no one consulted him about it. He felt he could have been someone great if only he had all of his thumbs.

You might think that living with Mrs. Capp has damaged my ego. After all, I am young, slim, in my prime. I should be the one waltzing off in tight pants on Friday nights. The messages on the phone pad should be for me. But in truth, I didn't move here to meet people. I came here to retreat. At some point last year, I realized that I didn't like many of my friends in California. They were just people living boring lives that seemed less boring because they were young and busy. But each of them toiled away at meaningless jobs, showered with water from the same treatment facility, had the same hurt feelings when their lovers broke their hearts.

It's not that I fancied myself different from them. It was that I began to see myself as indistinguishable. Rachel Rattford would order a turkey sandwich and I'd want the same thing. She'd buy new shoes and I'd have them already. Erica Wong would fight with her father and come over crying and I'd realize that I'd had that fight with my own father. Instead of making me feel comforted, one of a great community of souls, I found myself trying to pump up my experiences so that they'd look unique. I'd embellish my trip to the drugstore, reminding myself that I'd given a homeless woman my Belgian chocolates and faux diamond barrettes. I told Thomas that I saw a brown ring of what looked like lipstick smudged onto the floor in the center of the tampon aisle. I said it looked like a sign, a secret code left by a fugitive for his mate. A symbol that he was whole, alive, well.

"They never clean that store," Thomas replied.

And I understood what I was doing. This took most of the fun out of it.

The East Coast began to look like frontier—the new world beckoning to me with its welcoming, deeply lined hands. It was the only way to extricate myself from the excruciating plainness of my life—Thomas, the jars of chutney crystallizing in the fridge, the relentless Friday night parties where self-congratulatory med students and budding Ph.D.s got drunk on gin and pretended to forget the rules of social interaction.

Now I am three thousand miles away, eating pasta and canned tomatoes and picking my toenails while I read. And it's a constant reminder, watching Mrs. Capp fuss with her hair and apply too much rouge, that it's hell to care about the world the way she does.

Satan lingers in the doorway, grinning. "Well, come innn," Mrs. Capp coos. For a moment he's frozen in the sunlight, and then with a loping gait he follows her into the kitchen.

I should have known that she was up to something this morning. She was out of her quilted housedress when I woke up at nine and sharply attired in a pair of polyester slacks with navy blue flats and dark beige hose. She's got on a pair of earrings she bought recently. Large cloisonné ducks. They swing as she moves her thin neck.

I stop reading the paper and listen. Mrs. Capp puts her face in the freezer, and though it's difficult to hear what she's saying, I can hear the cadence of her fluty voice.

"Sure," Satan says. "Okay." Ice clanks. Some chairs move. The back door opens. Shuts.

I snort to myself. Satan as a Sunday morning visitor. It seems appropriately absurd. A blatant metaphor for why I don't date. Why I pour over the *Times* (alone) on Sunday mornings, plan my weekends according to books on my shelf, homework, walks, and movies I haven't yet seen. I enjoy the freedom of my newfound solitude. It's still a novelty.

The initial phases were harder. When the graduate school acceptance letter came through my mail slot one Tuesday morning, Thomas was in my kitchen, slurping cereal. I grabbed it out of the heap of bills and advertisements, ripped it open with my thumb. "As the competition this year was formidable, we are especially pleased to notify you…"

Thomas' face puckered when I showed it to him. "You're not going, are you?" I looked at his stubbly jaw, his mat of brown, coarse hair, the one eyebrow that stood up like it had suffered some great shock.

"I don't know," I said. Those words were a set of stairs that only went down.

Weeks later, during dinner at an overpriced Vietnamese restaurant, I broke the news. Women with luminous teeth and dark, glistening hair sat with men in button-down shirts, leather bags stashed neatly beside their chairs. "I've accepted the offer," I told him. I'd waited until this very public moment to tell him so that he couldn't throw a fit. I thought of the noodles caught in that silent mouth. He didn't chew. He just looked at me.

His brown eyes, so familiar, so expressive, were utterly blank. I cringed. I knew I'd made a terrible mistake, and one for which I wouldn't be forgiven. The mistake was not in leaving California. It was telling him here, like this, the smell of steamed mussels between us like a fog.

"Everything all right?" our waitress asked.

"Oh, it's delicious," I said. I wanted her to stay, to sit down with us and tell us funny stories about herself. "But I'd like a beer."

"And you?" she said, turning her unsuspecting gaze to Thomas. He continued to stare at me for a beat. The world went still. Then, his eyes began to tear, then gape, and his hands flew to his throat.

The waitress smiled patiently.

"Thomas?" I said. "Are you okay?" He opened his mouth and his face started turning a strange shade of red. Then redder. And in very little time, a deep shade of burgundy.

"He's choking!" I told the waitress.

The following minutes are somewhat blurry. I'd taken a CPR course but so long ago—when had I ever used it? And I'm ashamed to say that the only thing that came into my mind was that if Thomas died right then, I might be responsible for killing him; I was presumably the reason he choked, and I'd failed to perform the skills for which I'd been trained. I began to think of my defense. No one ever had to know that I'd chosen that minute to tell him I was leaving. I could claim it was one of those random horrors in life—a lover struck down by the gods in front of a beautiful meal. And while I was thinking this, the waitress began to pound on Thomas' back and then one of the glossy haired women at a nearby table ran over, grabbed the waitress's arm, wrenched it away, lifted Thomas to a vulnerable, half-upright position, hugged him from behind and BAM, out flew the wad of noodles onto the white tablecloth.

I dropped him off at his apartment and he got out of the car without kissing me. The relief I felt watching him go through the dirty glass doors into the foyer of his building has followed me out here. I'm still glad that Thomas is alive, those pink scars marking his lonely thumbs, the noodles out of his airways. But I'm also glad not to be with him, walking through the glass doors, up the ammonia-scented stairway to his one-bedroom apartment.

Mrs. Capp and Satan are on the porch drinking lemonade. If I sit on my bed, in the corner of the room, I can see them through the window. And because the windows are so old, the seals broken, the glass rattling in strong wind, I can hear most of what they're saying.

"It's terrible to lose someone," I hear Satan say.

"It is," Mrs. Capp says sadly. "It's like the world is whisked away from you. Nothing looks the same."

Satan grunts. Mrs. Capp must recognize the irony of explaining loss to Satan but it doesn't show on her face.

What thoughts are flashing through his mind? Is he truly sympathetic or is it a ruse to get what he wants?

"I brought you a present," Satan says, gesturing to a small pink package. She gazes at it as if it were the correct ending to her sad thoughts. She's holding the package on her lap and I'm annoyed that I can't see what's inside when she carefully edges off the foil.

What gift does Satan bring on a Sunday morning? Apple chips? Tarot cards? Snakeskin barrettes?

"So sweet," she croons. She gets up, sits in his lap, and gives him a long, passionate kiss. She pulls away and Satan looks at her in the same way he looked at the headline on the paper. She rakes her pearly nails down the edge of his jaw, stands, gathers the empty glasses. I hear the back door open.

I jump off my bed, smooth out the wrinkles in my quilt. She pokes her head in.

"He's cute, isn't he?"

"Yeah," I say. "Sure." The canned innocence of my voice is a giveaway that I've been spying but she's too preoccupied to notice.

"Oh, gosh, Liza. Come outside and talk to him. I've got a really strong feeling about this one."

When Mrs. Capp talks about men, she sounds as if she's dangling from a fine thread. She seems frightened of falling. Maybe this is why she lines them up one after the other: the next one can catch her if the thread snaps.

She goes out into the kitchen to refill their glasses. I yank off my pajamas and slide into the jeans and sweater I left by my bed the night before. Outside, the backyard is brimming with life. The brown grass is turning green again. The large oak tree has its first leaves. Satan smiles at me. I pull up a chair.

"How's it going?" I ask. I can tell from the lack of sheen on his eyes that he doesn't really want me to be there.

"Good," he says, wiping the edge of his lip. His limbs are excessively long in comparison to his compact torso. And he's not particularly good-looking. There's a lack of symmetry to his face. His eyes are crooked and small and his mouth and nose are squishy. All of this under a giant forehead, his hairline receding.

Mrs. Capp flings herself through the door, her face a cramped expression of joy. She's brought me a lemonade, as well.

"Satan's a house painter," Mrs. Capp says to me as she settles onto her chair. He nods.

"I was just telling him that our house could use a little painting." This is true. The peach paint is peeling in the front and half the window frames are a glossy maroon while the other half are dirty white.

"Sure," he says, his voice surprisingly gravelly. "We could probably work out a trade." He directs this statement to Mrs. Capp and his head lowers slightly. His lids drop over those small blue eyes. Mrs. Capp shoots him a reprimanding glance but lightens it with a purse of her lips, which, I notice, have a fresh coat of magenta lipstick.

Satan leans back in his chair and parts his legs. His hands dangle between his thighs. I catch a whiff of his smell. It's animal—dank and cit-rus at once, musky and a little dizzying—the kind of body odor you can't help breathing in repeatedly, though it seems inappropriate to do so.

There's a rising tide of energy at the table and it's making me uncom-fortable. It seems that at any moment, Satan might lunge over the patio table with no regard to the tall glasses of lemonade, grasp Mrs. Capp with his clearly capable hands and mash those soft features into her powdered neckline.

"So, how'd you get your name?" I ask. A chill comes over the porch. Satan doesn't take his eyes off Mrs. Capp. He's got the fingers of both hands pressed together and he's doing little push-ups with them. No one has anything to say.

I have never had any illusions about knowing the workings of Mrs. Capp's soul but right now I feel particularly alienated. In my head I list what I know to be true: She likes all-natural peanut butter (no salt); light blue is her favorite color; she keeps her jewelry in a glass box etched with a picture of the night sky. I realized that she was a little bit desperate but there's an edginess to her need I wasn't aware of before.

Her neck suddenly looks more than thin; it seems breakable. A frag-ile twig in a huge storm.

"We were thinking of going to a matinee," Mrs. Capp says. She wrin-kles her eyes and nose into some sort of smile.

"What movie?" I ask. Really, I couldn't care less. I want to know where Satan was born, under what awful sky.

"Whatever's playing," she says.

I take the last cookie from the fancy platter on the table. Beside the platter is the CD Satan brought for Mrs. Capp in that pink foil. It's called, *Music for the Living: Experiments in Joyful Sound*. That's just too much. Who is he trying to fool?

There's a shifting under the table. Satan's foot, clad in a dirty Converse high-top, is creeping up Mrs. Capp's leg and his knee, in the process, is bumping against my thigh. I set the CD down with a thwack. Mrs. Capp raises her eyebrows.

"Well," she says, "if we're going to go, I should put on a warmer sweater. I always get cold in theaters." She takes the CD and places it on the empty platter. Satan gathers the glasses and follows her into the house. I stay outside, looking at the oak tree trembling in the imperceptible wind.

After a few minutes, I get up and walk around the house. A large Dodge van is parked out front. Satan's van. The windows are tinted and a large, expandable ladder is secured to the top of it. There's a big dent in the rear bumper. I circle the van and I'm surprised to find a mural painted on the door of the driver's side. It's a crudely painted picture of the planet earth. The continents make a green/brown yin-yang with the bright blue ocean. Underneath it is a red heart with the words ONE LOVE printed inside. The rest of the van is a sinister gray with a black stripe running along the base. I stand on my tiptoes and peer into the back. It's as I suspected. Among some paint cans and roller brushes is a foam mattress with a flannel sleeping bag. A tapestry is fastened to the ceiling.

Who is this man? Where did he come from? How long is he going to stay? Should I be concerned about my stuff?

For the first time since I moved here, I feel distinctly alone. Not solitary, but unseen. I don't miss anyone, exactly. Who would I miss? If Thomas were here he would claim to know things he didn't know. He would say that none of this was our business. He would shrug and suggest that we play ultimate frisbee in the dog park.

Plates in my chest are shifting, opening a wide crevasse. People fill these chasms with people. They cram them full of friends, lovers, parents, siblings, unrequited crushes. They drown out the gaping silence with the noise of various lives. But all things gained cost something; this filling of a void is at the expense of one's own clattering hush. The hush is what I wanted. It's what I moved here for.

The street is quiet. I can hear the movement of blood through my body. I look at the peeling peach house in front of me and kick the tire of the van. Nothing happens. The feeling is lodged there, disconcerting, a noisy stinging in my chest.

I go back inside. The door to Mrs. Capp's room is shut. I stand in front of it, staring at the white paint. I wonder if they've managed to leave without letting me know. This seems unlikely. Mrs. Capp doesn't have a car and the bus stop is right across the street. Then, I hear a giggle. Several giggles, a moan.

I know I should leave. I'm crossing a line by standing here in front of her door. I should go back into my bedroom, read a magazine. Then there is a creaking sound. Some talking. I get even closer, put my ear up to the crack.

"Oh, that's so strange," she says. Her voice sounds husky, playful. "Stoppit!" There's a cracking sound, like a horsewhip. A squeal.

"Like this," he says. And then the words are muffled.

"Oh God!" she cries. The sound of rustling. "Ohhh, Satan." Relative silence. Soon, a rhythmic thudding begins. I back away and walk aimlessly into the kitchen.

Eavesdropping has only intensified the bad feeling. I can't think of a single thing to do. Satan's denim jacket is draped on a chair. A pack of cigarettes pokes from the top pocket. I take one with the matchbook and go out onto the porch. Mrs. Capp would throw a fit if she saw me smoking but it seems safe to assume she's preoccupied. I inspect the matchbook, hoping it's from an incriminating place—a strip joint or casino. But the matchbook just advertises a brand of cigarettes. The light is pretty through the tree and the spring air feels cold but alive on my face. I will a silence to take over my thoughts, but before I'm even finished with the cigarette, a voice comes from behind me.

"She's a fine woman, that Sondra." My heart skips, then a hot surge of blood races to my ears. He's standing in the doorway. I turn to see him adjust his privates through the canvas of his pants. He's so efficient. A real time manager. If he worked a service job, his face would be lacquered to a celebratory plaque. "Satan! Never A Moment Wasted!"

It takes me a moment to register what he's just said. Fine woman. Who says "fine woman"? What could that possibly mean? Is it a euphemism for a good, easy lay? And he called her Sondra. I don't think I've ever heard anyone call her Sondra. Not even her mail comes addressed like that. Each piece of it simply calls for Mrs. Capp. Not Mrs. Sondra Capp or Mrs. S. Capp. She's not a first name woman; I don't care how "fine" she is. I feel myself developing a glare and I turn it on Satan. He's oblivious.

"Really a first-class broad," he says. He can't be serious. He must be trying to get my goat. But he doesn't appear ironic. He lights a cigarette and leans lazily against the door frame, crossing his gangly legs.

I try to think of a decent retort. It doesn't have to be a good one, any one will do, but I'm so miffed I can't even put together a subject and a verb. Mrs. Capp walks out.

"Liza, dear, do you think you can help me find my keys?" This must be a cue: She wants to conspire with me to get rid of Satan. She realizes she's slipped and now she wants a trusty female hand out of the mess. I stamp out the cigarette and breathe deeply. Mrs. Capp turns and I see Satan run a hand up the back of her leg and goose her. She ducks and swats at his hand, giggles. He grins.

Inside the living room, Mrs. Capp begins to root around between the sofa cushions. I stand next to her dumbly, waiting for her to say something.

"Could you check around, dear?" she says. "Maybe they're underneath a magazine or something." I halfheartedly pick up the paper. Nothing. Carefully, I fold it along its creases and set it on top of the unread sections on the coffee table. Mrs. Capp is scurrying about, lifting picture frames off the mantle, patting pillows, straightening up as she looks.

"Maybe you left them in a pocket," I suggest.

"Well, it seems unlikely," she says. "But let's check." I follow her into her bedroom and almost keel over, the smell of sex is so strong. Her powder blue curtains are drawn and the bedsheets are tangled. Her fluffy comforter is pushed to one side and a condom wrapper lays torn and empty by the foot of the bed. She doesn't notice my obvious discomfort. With a swift movement she scoops up the comforter and settles it back on the bed. I walk stiffly to her dresser and peer at the contents. There are the cloisonné ducks. This comforts me. She does seem the sort to take her jewelry off before a romp in the sack. I touch the earrings. They're cold and hard. I press the little hooks into my thumb as I mentally archive the rest of her belongings. The etched night sky box. A little glass paperweight with a miniature seal caught inside. A crocheted doily, slightly stained, with a framed photograph of Mrs. Capp's deceased parents on top of it. They look normal enough in the photo. Her father is in military uniform, a moustache falling over his lip, a cap shadowing his face. Her mother stands erect by his side, unsmiling, her eyebrows a straight line across her forehead.

"Where on earth could they be?" she says. Then she sees the condom wrapper and picks it off the ground, sticks it in her pocket. She meets my eyes and blushes slightly. I feel emboldened.

"I just think you should know," I say, "when you were inside, Satan called you a first-class broad." That ought to shock her. A broad. Where does he get off?

"Well, isn't that sweet," she says, that perky uplift to her voice. I study her face. Surely it's going to fall into something other than that dreamy smile.

"I told you, Liza, he's special. I can sense it."

"That's one way to look at it." I jam the hook into my thumb a little harder.

Mrs. Capp doesn't seem to see Satan at all. Maybe she only sees MAN, the potential of that gender, the filling of a slot that is currently empty. I suppose, if this is her route through life, double thumbs and other realities would only throw her off track.

While Mrs. Capp goes through her jacket pockets, I try to imagine what my life would have been like had I followed Thomas up those stairs, into that dim apartment. He would have sulked for a while about his potential death while the sky outside darkened to black. I would have sat on the scratchy wool sofa, paging through a copy of *The Green Planet* or some weathered high school English novel Thomas kept on his bookshelf for show. He would have taken a shower, emerged wet and sullen, his brown hair sticking up in shiny cowlicks all over his scalp. Soon he would have nestled next to me, buried his face in my neck, forgiven me my lack of heroism, forgiven God for nearly killing him. We could have gone on like that, the scratchy sofa bothering our legs, into the great infinity. Would that really have been so bad?

"Here they are!" Mrs. Capp says. If the keys had hair, she'd give it a good-natured tousle. "They must have fallen off the night table." She jiggles them in her palm. Little castanets.

Mrs. Capp is going out with Satan. This is what she wants. I sit down on the bed and smile.

"Don't do anything I wouldn't do," I tell her. She winks at me.

"Oh Liza," she says. "You wouldn't do anything."

THE
BEADS

I NEVER LIKED THE STAINED GLASS THAT WOUND AROUND THE top of the synagogue walls. Even when I was young, the right age to be mesmerized by such things, it seemed out of place. Color like that belonged in candy or painted on the front of vacation tee shirts. The glass was set into triangles and circles that went from large to small, making trippy little stars of David, triangular sun rays, and the occasional cluster of purple grapes.

At my mother's memorial service, I stared at the patterns the sun cast on the linoleum. Each time someone went up to the bema to read a poem or recite an overly rehearsed anecdote about my mother's life, I tried to find the corresponding blob. Pilar, my mother's law partner who cried like her fingers were jammed in the door, got the large blue smear. Zoe, a doughy woman from her cancer support group got the weak yellow parallelogram. My father stood on one side of me, my boyfriend, Kevin, on the other. Every time one of my mother's friends got up to say something, I felt more and more dangerous, as if it would take only one more thing to make those blobs of color harden into weapons I could lob at them.

"It's not like it'll do me much good when I'm dead, dear." Her voice was wry as she gestured to her legs, two small ridges beneath the tangle of sheets and quilts. "It's a shitty body—it's been useless for years." My mother had been a good criminal lawyer. I'd grown up believing that abductions and drug trafficking were a mundane part of life—she could discuss them in the same blithe way she could discuss what sort of melons the farmer's market had that day.

My father brought home paperwork and I pretended to watch television as my mother signed the forms. It was bad enough she was dying. It was hard to get my head around the idea of her life disappearing, of her no longer sitting in the bed, gasping for air, asking after my friends and giving strict orders about dinner preparations. But to imagine her body in pieces—

It wasn't as if her organs were any good. She wouldn't continue to live in the grateful bodies of strangers. The cancer was in her bones, her liver. The radiation had damaged her heart and lungs. She'd simply be a specimen. Her mutant cells. Her paralyzed diaphragm. "This is one mess of a woman," the student would say, lifting her liver to the glare of a lab light.

As we stood under the rainbow sunlight at the memorial service, I thought of my mother on a gleaming metal table.

Kevin drove the car back to my house after the reception.

"It was a really nice service," he said, reaching over to touch my hair.

"It didn't feel like a service," I said, toying with the handle of the door. "How can there be a funeral without a body?"

Kevin was quiet. Several weeks before this, I'd gone to get a shirt out of one of his drawers and I'd found a stack of grief and loss books hidden there. When he took a shower that night, I thumbed through them. What could he possibly learn from these books? Would they tell him about the strange, hue-less colors in my mind at night, the feeling of dangling over a giant maw, no bottom in sight?

"I love you, Yael," he said. His words floated around the car, looking for a place to land.

I went to my father's place almost daily in the week following the service. We sipped Scotch on the couch in the apartment that he rented when my mother went into hospice. We didn't talk much. We were both waiting for the next phase to engulf us. She'd been alive a moment ago, her brown eyes a little childlike, a little deranged from all the pain. She'd been on oxygen and on morphine in those last weeks, but her realness, her heat made the impending absence abstract. I could still lay a hand on her chest, feel the warmth through her blue nightgown. I knew her, and somewhere in that muddled mess of her mind, I was her child. But now she wasn't there to touch. And she didn't feel gone. So my father and I were left to navigate that fragment of a world between the dying and the dead.

One night, about a week after the service, he called.

"Yael, I've got some strange news." He was using his doctor voice. Clipped and clinical. "I just got a call from the lab." My heart soared. It wasn't my mother who died! (I knew it!) She was sitting on a beach in Maine eating cherries! She was coming home!

"They've done some work on her cadaver and—" Cadaver. A brick landed in my chest. "It seems that your mother's stomach was full of beads."

"Beads?"

"Beads," he said. "Very strange."

I drove down to his apartment. It had large gates in front and a lit-up box where you punched in an access code. He was pacing outside the door when I pulled up. I gave him a quick hug and walked inside. There on the dining room table in a gallon zip-lock bag were the beads, about the size of popcorn kernels. Most of them were round, though some were shaped more like cocoons. Some were brightly colored—blues, purples, yellows, a glossy green, a bloody scarlet. Others looked like antique bone or dirty stucco.

I scooped some up and a few fell to the carpet. It was like reaching into the loose gravel of a river bottom—cold and clean. I tried to imagine my mother full of them. A strange weight. If her skin were translucent she would have looked like stained glass, like the synagogue window. My father breezed behind me on the way to the kitchen.

"I'm having a Scotch," he said. "You want one?"

We sat on the living room floor, sipping from the tumblers, staring at beads glittering under the track lighting.

I couldn't remember my mother ever wearing beads. She'd been raised in Brooklyn and despite my parents' migration to California in the 1970s, she'd never gotten hip to the bohemian thing. She liked gold jewelry. Classy little hoops hooked into her ears. A delicate gold band on her ring finger.

My mother was a woman devoid of fancy. She felt no remorse as she threw out my childhood paintings or my father's love letters. She bought tuna fish on sale and bulk flour. Did she secretly long for color and excess? Did a bead bloom each time she wished for a silk scarf or expensive underwear? Or did the beads have to do with the cancer? For every bad cell her body produced an apology in the form of a small glass bead. Her body knew it wouldn't survive; it would have to give itself over to the earth or to a yellow incinerator bag, so it had produced these objects that might outlast it.

Finally, my father spoke. "She must have eaten them," he said.

My father was a doctor, after all, and so the world revealed itself to him in an orderly fashion. There were things that were possible and things that were not. I reached out for a green bead and held it to the light.

"Why would she have done that?" I asked.

"We'll never know," he said gravely.

I knew this was absurd. My mother disliked all things strange. She was a finicky eater. And she'd been in the hospital for weeks before she died, getting fluid from an IV. Who would have fed her beads?

My father wiped a tear from his cheek and I felt an unbearable aching in my chest, creeping up into my throat. I put the bead back and held him in a clumsy embrace.

"I'm getting rid of them," he said. I let go of him and took the bag.

"No, I'll take them," I said. "We can decide what to do with them when things calm down." My father nodded absently and rubbed the back of his neck.

Kevin stood in my small bathroom, looking at the beads. I'd rinsed them off and put them in a metal mixing bowl. He was twirling a piece of his dark hair, something he did when he puzzled over crosswords or talked to a difficult editor on the phone. I understood that my mother's death was taking its toll on him. He was used to my staying up late with him, formulating good interview questions, helping him with his articles. I could tell that he didn't know what his role was supposed to be now that death had made an entrance, now that I carried this somber knowledge, a password to a world he couldn't enter. He'd been growing more and more awkward, touching my back with a nervous palm, looking at me with a mix of empathy and impatience.

"It's got to be a sick joke," Kevin said, padding back into my bedroom. He sat on the bed. "That's just too fucked up."

"A joke?" I asked.

"I don't know. Maybe there's some sort of pathology lab fraternity brotherhood or something."

I got off the bed where I'd been waiting for him.

"What?" he said. "You think all those beads just magically appeared inside your mother?"

I walked into the bathroom, locked the door, turned off the light, and shoved my hand deep into the bowl. The beads were cool and heavy. I wished there were enough of them to fill the bathtub. I'd have slept in them.

"Yael," Kevin called. "Are you okay?"

I took a bead in between my thumb and forefinger. I could make out, though the room was dark, a slight red sheen. I slipped it into my mouth and swallowed.

"Yael," Kevin said, his voice grave, authoritative. "Please open the door."

I unlocked it and the doorknob turned. His eyebrows were drawn close to his buggy eyes and his mouth turned down in perplexed pout. I let him pull me towards him. The shampoo in his hair smelled like pears, and mixed with that, the faint, animal smell of his scalp.

My mother is dead, I said to myself. But the words sounded ridiculous. Kevin is trying to help me because my mother is dead. I pushed him aside and climbed into bed.

"I'm exhausted," I said. But really I just wanted to close my eyes. I wanted to see if I could feel it, that shiny red bead, slipping silently through me.

When the alarm went off, I woke feeling strangely elated.

"Kev," I whispered. I could tell he was awake. I shoved my foot between his ankles and felt his scratchy leg hairs. "Wake up." I ran a hand down his chest, hooked a finger in the elastic of his boxers, scooted close. He opened one eye.

"What time is it?" He lifted his head to look at the clock and groaned. "I have that meeting at eight-thirty," he said. "Those masochists."

Kevin and I left one another alone in the mornings. We both hated the violence of waking, hated each and every bird that chirped. But this morning the sun was coming right out of the center of my stomach. Kevin made a move to get out of bed, but I crooked my arm around his neck and dragged him toward me. I felt radiant, zinging with life. I put his hand on my chest.

"Are you okay?" he asked.

"Yes," I said, rolling on top of him. "I'm good." I tugged down his boxers.

After he left, vaguely puzzled and disheveled, I carried the bowl of beads to the coffee table. I gathered the necessary materials. Dental floss. A sewing needle. I watched the beads gather on the string. I tied the necklace off and hung it around my neck. It hit just over my heart.

I'd forgotten about it by the time Kevin got home. He came into the house, set his bag down by the coffee table, and was going into the kitchen when he stopped short.

"You made a necklace?" His eyes were wide, his brows little umbrellas of alarm. And then his nose wrinkled in disgust. I fingered the beads. Red, dirty bone, blue, green, clear.

"They're beautiful," I said.

Kevin shook his head and raised his arms a little, then dropped them to his side heavily. "Yael," he said, squinting a little. "That's just messed up."

"I think they're beautiful."

"Those beads," Kevin started, and then shook his head. His voice was loud, higher pitched than usual. "Those beads were sitting in your mother's stomach!" Kevin squinted. He was waiting for me to get it, to take the necklace off and hurl it onto the carpet as if it were a snake. I put my hand over the beads.

"DO YOU NOT SEE THAT THAT'S DISTURBING?"

"You said you thought it was a joke," I said.

Kevin continued to shake his head. "I don't know how to deal with this," he said, and stormed past me, through the dining room, out to the patio.

I closed my eyes and tried to feel what I felt. When I went out, he was crying.

"Maybe it's too hard," he said, covering his face with his hands. "Maybe I just can't take it." I knelt down next to the chair where he was sitting.

"I don't know what you want from me," he continued. "I don't know what I can give you." A fresh wave of sobs washed over him.

In the dimming light of the summer sky the beads looked almost supernatural, like a wad of colored foil burned in the center of each one. I could feel the weight of the glass around my neck.

"It's just so much pressure," he said. I looked out into the trees behind my building. It was almost dusk and they cast strange shadows over the lawn. Again, I shut my eyes. This time, though, I felt peace. It seemed to begin right where the necklace fell over my chest, spreading through my body like a vapor. I put a hand on Kevin's arm. Then I stood, sat in his lap, and cradled his head to my breast.

"Please take the beads off," he said. I'd climbed in bed next to him in my nightgown. The beads hung beneath the thin fabric, making a ridge.

"No," I said. "They give me comfort." I hadn't expected to say this, but after I did, I realized it was true. I was never going to take them off.

Kevin rolled onto his back and breathed deeply. "Don't I give you comfort?" he asked.

"Of course you give me comfort," I said.

Kevin turned to face me. "I'm not sure I do," he said. And then he rolled over.

I couldn't sleep. If they had found these beads in my mother's stomach, then wasn't it possible they'd find other things inside her as well? Keys? Scrolls? Tiny mirrors? I crawled out of bed and went into the living room to call my father.

"Hello!" His voice was tired and alarmed.

"Sorry. I can't sleep." He sighed. I had never done this before. My father, a heart doctor, had always been greedy about his rest.

"I can't sleep either," he said. "I've been feeling very odd."

"Odd how?" I asked.

"Do you have the beads?" he asked.

"Yeah."

"Good. Don't throw them out," he said. "I think we should keep them in the family." And then, out of nowhere, "Yael, actually—do you think I could come over and take a look at them?"

"Now?" I asked.

"If that's okay. I know it's late, but I can't sleep either."

Twenty minutes later, my father knocked softly on the front door. The whites of his eyes were tinged with red and in the corners a yellow gel seemed to be gathering. He grabbed my shoulders stiffly and pulled me forward. I tried to lean into the embrace but it put me off balance. I led him into the living room. The bowl of beads sat on the coffee table. I'd put on my robe, careful to make sure he couldn't see the necklace.

He walked over and knelt in front of them.

"I don't understand," he said, putting his large, hairy hand deep into the bowl of beads. And then his face went still. The muscles in his jaw pulled back, his nostrils bent toward his mouth which opened a crack, pulled down. He started to wail. He was rocking back and forth, grasping his shoulders with his hands, kneading at himself as if aiming for balance. Each time he bent forward, the cries got louder, and as he rocked back, the tone would change to a higher pitch. It went on and on without breath, miraculously continuous.

Kevin came padding out of the bedroom. He looked at me, alarmed. I looked at my father. I'd heard stories about grieving. Women threw themselves on the graves of their dead husbands, their eyes rolled back, their throats dilated. The noise they made came from some lost part of the human soul. But I hadn't expected this from my father. When my mother finally stopped breathing, he put his hand on her head then pulled the sheet over her face. He called the attending nurse. He made sure the right papers were signed.

And then the wailing stopped. The room went quiet. For a moment, I could feel the small hairs on my neck, my arms. Then my father hung his head, balled his hands into fists, and wept. I knelt next to him. Kevin followed and knelt next to me. I put my hand on my father's back. Kevin put his hand on my back. And we just sat there, listening to my father cry. He took some deep breaths.

"I'm sorry," he said. "I'm sorry."

I shook my head and patted his back.

"Don't be sorry," Kevin said. And my father began crying again.

I brought out extra sheets and blankets and put my father to bed on the sofa.

"How are you?" Kevin asked. He was standing in front of me in the bedroom. His brown eyes were lit with a sympathy that seemed to me to be perpetually there, perpetually feigned. His face was familiar—those long, girlish lashes, bruised-looking lips, a scar from a dog bite on his jaw. I tried to imagine what he thought I must feel. Did my grief look like grief? The thought was infuriating. He set his chin on my head.

"I don't know," I said. I fumbled for the necklace and grasped the beads in my hand. They were warm from my skin, animal and alive, as if inside each of them beat a tiny little heart.

When I woke up, my father was on the sofa drinking coffee. Kevin had already left for work.

"I'm sorry about last night," he said. His face was an old man's face. There was a gray tint to his skin and his sideburns were completely white. He used to look tall and brusque, always rushing away in dark, polished shoes. But now he wore gray sneakers and he looked wilted and frail.

"Don't be," I said. I went and sat next to him. My heart felt large and soft. I put a hand on his arm. And then his eyes locked on my neck. I touched the beads. Instead of accusing me of mental illness, yelling at me for my vanity, he averted his eyes. He stared deep into the mug of coffee.

"I made plans to go sailing today," he said. "I'm trying to get out of the house."

"That's good," I said. But my mind wasn't linking up to the present. I could only feel the beads beneath my fingers.

"I'm going with a woman from the hospital, but I just want you to know that it's not really a date." I looked at him, still staring at the coffee.

"It's not a date," I repeated.

"Of course not," he said. "How could it be a date?"

"How could it be a date?"

"How could it be?" he said.

Every cell of my body suddenly got heavy. A date? It had occurred to me that this would happen someday, but not a week after her death. She'd been sick for years, dying for months, but her death was new. It was like a magic trick, of sorts: now you see mom in the bed, now you see a bed!

"I can't believe this."

"What?"

"I can't believe you'd even think of dating right now." My body was glued to the sofa but my head was about to go reeling off my body, spinning wildly around the room, shrieking and cursing.

"I just told you it isn't a date," he said.

"She just died!"

"Yael, this is hard for me," he said. "I know it's hard for you, too. But I need to do something. I need to get out. I can't spend my days locked in the house, feeling that I never knew how to be happy and now I never will—"

Happy? Of course he wasn't happy. They'd been married thirty years and now she was dead. Why would he be happy? And that he'd never been happy? Happy was word to be squished through the nose at birthday parties. Happy!

"There's a lot you don't know," he said. "Your mother and I were our own people, not just your parents."

"Please leave," I said. I stood and walked toward the door. My father looked cowed. He set the coffee cup down on the table, picked up his coat, and walked toward me.

"I'm only trying to be honest," he said.

A feverish heat washed over me. As he wailed the night before, I'd hoped he'd stop. But now I wanted to switch the flip, watch him howl and bawl every day for the rest of his life. We'd take each bead and recount a memory of my mother: the way she tapped each dish after she washed it; how she'd scamper to get the paper in the morning, still in her nightgown, her hair sticking up, her cheeks creased—and as we talked, we'd drown in borderless, limitless grief. When we got to the last bead, we'd start again.

"Go be honest somewhere else," I said.

I was supposed to meet Kevin for lunch downtown but now I had no interest in walking to the train. I didn't want to see him—his cleanly shaved jaw, his well-meaning eyes. I only wanted to see him if his mother were dead. I only wanted friends with dead parents. I'd start a club. Maybe even a commune. I'd surround myself with people who would promise NEVER to say the word happy, who wouldn't use any of its synonyms. We'd be like an experimental French novel. No version of joy ever. We wouldn't even use the letters of happy. No H. No A. No P. No Y.

The phone rang and the machine picked up. No one left a message. The phone started up again. I got up, stumbled over to it.

"What," I said. I was crying.

"Jesus, Yael?" Kevin sounded concerned. "I don't suppose you're coming for lunch? I just called to tell you I made reservations at that Japanese place, but—another time. I'll just come home. Are you okay?"

Okay? Was okay like happy?

"Of course not." I hung up.

In the bathroom, the tiles were cold beneath my feet. I filled the tub.

Then I dumped the beads into it. If you cry enough, you can get to that still place the yoga people are always talking about. I was calmer. But I felt tired. Cloudlike. Empty. I took off my nightgown and stood watching the water rise.

It roared out of the tap. The beads gathered near the drain, a colorful smattering of glass, brighter beneath the water. They looked odd against the porcelain. I put one foot in. It was scalding.

I sat until the water was cool. I gazed at the light blue ceiling, the small crack that led from the window above the tub to the corner of the room.

Keys jangled and the front door slammed.

"Yael?" Kevin called, walking toward our bedroom. I was getting a chill but I didn't want to move. I rolled the beads under my feet and stared at the shower curtain around me. A small vine of orange mold had started at the bottom of one of the curtains and was clinging toward the edge of it. Rust spotted the metal at the top of the rod.

"Hey," he said coming into the bathroom. He sat on the toilet and peered at me. My eyes felt dry, the skin around them thin and tattered.

"How are you doing?"

"Fantastic," I said. "Never better."

"Okay," he said. There it was again, that stupid, stupid word. He reached over and tucked a wet strand of hair behind my ear. His hand lingered there. I put my hand on his for a moment then pushed it away.

"I brought you some food from that soul food place on the corner," he said.

I didn't want to look at him. I stared at the rust growths. They looked like starfish.

He sighed. "Yael, you gotta help me out here. I'm doing the best I can."

This was Kevin's burden? Was I supposed to comfort him? Oh Kevin, I'll be alright. It only takes six weeks of grieving and I'll be over it!

"Fuck off," I said.

"Oh, that's really nice. I bring you lunch while you're acting like a total psychopath, rolling around in your mother's stomach remnants, and you tell ME to fuck off. You fuck off." He continued to sit on the toilet. Why didn't he just leave? My insides were made of lint and tiny red embers, a combustible combination of stillness and fury. He ought to get out now and find himself a nice girl with two functional parents and maybe a little dog to play with in the park. He'd like that.

"I'm not getting out," I said.

Kevin looked down at his shoes. Brown leather loafers, appropriate for a budding journalist. News shoes. The toes were worn, the rubber soles curving a bit at the heels. He stood, took the bag of food, and walked out of the bathroom.

I thought I'd hear him leave. I waited for the door to slam but it didn't. He'd gone into the kitchen. I could hear the cupboards opening. I sank down into the tub and submerged myself—but as my head went under, I had to bend my knees more and they stuck out of the water. I sat back up, my head soaked, my knees cold, and started to shiver.

Kevin came back into the bathroom holding my old bathrobe and the beach towel. "Get out," he said. His voice was gentle. His face was expressionless. I looked at him.

"I'm not ready to get out," I said.

"Get out anyway."

An order. That was kind of exciting. No one had told me what to do in months, since my mother had been given her final prognosis. Everyone just nodded at everything I said or did. If they did ask things, they did it gently. I was an ominous force, a person to be pleaded with. I grasped the porcelain lip of the tub and raised myself out. I'd lost weight. My hip bones jutted out like fins near my sunken stomach. I stepped onto the bath mat, shaking now, and Kevin wrapped the towel around me, rubbed me down, held out the robe. We didn't speak. In the bedroom, I saw that he'd set all the food out on a silver baking pan. A yellow flower from the yard leaned in a large water glass. The ribs looked varnished, the potatoes like plastic. My stomach growled.

We got under the covers silently, Kevin gently situating the tray between us as if it were a small child. The gnawing in my stomach felt surprisingly good. An angry, painful little life. Kevin took a rib and started eating. He was careful not to look at me. He was staring at himself in the mirror across the room. I watched him chew. My wet hair hung in small snakes against my face. Against my pale skin, the beads were alarmingly bright. I touched them, held them. The tightness in my chest increased; it was hard to breathe.

In the mirror, the beads were full of an odd, beautiful light. I clutched at them, clung to them, pulled them forward with my sobs.

Kevin continued to eat while I cried, and for this I was thankful. If he'd asked me to talk to him, I would have had to admit that I knew she was dead, that no amount of piecing her back together would change that. We were left behind, my father and I. She's dead, I would have said to him. And it would have been as if she was on the floor below, her body stiffening, her hair thin from chemo, her mouth cracked open slightly as if trying to let in that last breath of air.

DATE

YOU'VE NEVER MET ANYONE LIKE THIS BEFORE. WHEN HE SPEAKS, which is not often, the letters come out of his mouth on a thin gold chain. He's embarrassed by this, but you find it charming. Sheepishly, he gathers the chains of letters and hooks the ends together, links them around your neck or your wrists. You've begun to look like a belly dancer, covered in ornaments; you glitter like a sunken treasure, a chest of gold coins.

You like the way you look, ensconced in his letters. Each time he leans across the table to bejewel you, you feel like a Christmas tree. You are Jewish and this is not a familiar feeling. You smile coyly.

All the other men you've met this year talk too much. Their words demand. They speak of ex-girlfriends and hikes they've enjoyed and movies with blond actresses and short, winning men and every sentence they speak feels like a staircase you're being asked to climb.

Not so this time. Now you sit in a dim bar with lacquered wooden tables and you can relax. You don't ask questions. You communicate through the muscles of your face. You sip gin through small stirring straws. And every once in a while, he looks like he is struggling to rise to the surface of a body of water and he heaves out a sentence. You look pretty in that color, he says. The words pain him; it looks like they must be sharp in his tubes, scraping him on their way up and out. You wear that sentence around your wrist. When you lift your hand to wipe your brow, you can see it sparkle though the bar is dark. It's cold in here you wear around your left ankle. Would you like to see my apartment you wear with pride around your neck.

His apartment is spare and clean. It's a studio with exposed brick and dark wood floors and a fireplace in which he has placed potted plants. There are no photographs or tennis shoes or books. Just a bed with white blankets and two red oil paintings on the wall. He pours you a glass of wine. You sit on the white sofa and stare out the giant windows that overlook a narrow street. You are high up above the small trees. The lights in neighboring buildings shine yellow and sad. The room smells empty, like eastern woods in winter.

He is a beautiful man. His eyebrows are thick and his cheekbones are high and there is a stoop to his stance. He makes you want to touch him.

He doesn't say things like you are so beautiful or you really turn me on, baby, or how do I unhook this? You put an arm around his neck and he kisses you. It feels like you are climbing into a hot bath—your entire body gives. His hands are at your blouse, his hands are at the zipper of your pants, he seems to have ten hands and soon you are on the white bed in nothing but gold chains, your hair dark against the white pillows, his eyes whirling and twirling.

You could be sleeping with a marble statue or a dream. You could be sleeping with a king or a famous painter or a god. You could be sleeping with anyone; his body is perfect and hairless and copper all over.

He is strong and desperate in bed and you pull at his hair and he arches his neck and his teeth bite at your jaw and your collarbone and then they bite at the necklaces and he yanks his head and one of them breaks. You feel breathless; you feel like the air is making you drunk. He smells like soil when you dig deep enough.

He picks you up and pins you to the wall above the bed. You feel as light as a bundle of twigs. His hands are traveling the length of your torso, he is pressing you up against the white walls as if he is going to hammer you up with the paintings.

You grab back at him. Your hands are warm and limber and there is a melted butter feeling in your legs that, with the drunken air, is making you feel reckless, is making you feel like you might do anything. You expect him to rise up between your legs and take you violently, but this is not what happens.

As his hands move over your body, you bury your face between his neck and shoulder. And when you finally pull back—because his hands have stopped around your throat—you are shocked to see his face. His eyes have lost the whirling. His mouth is agape. He looks trapped, terrified, unable to cry for help. You feel him grip the necklaces and yank. Pain bites your neck as the chains cut into your skin and the necklaces snap off. He holds them in his hands and then tosses them to the floor. They don't make a sound when they hit.

Then he goes for your wrists. He tears the bracelets off and you feel weight in all the spots in your body that are usually air. You want these bracelets; you want these necklaces. He tears off the anklets too and now you are just your skin and your hair and your bones and you realize how cold you are.

THE
MERCY BABY

I'T'S NOT THE BEST WAY TO LIVE. JESSE KNOWS THIS. AND HE knows that when people walk into the Town-n-Country Mart, they don't see him the way he sees himself or the way he would ever wish to be seen—as a person connected to his life by complicated circuitry, as a man with a hot, humming sting below his heart. When they breeze through the double glass doors to buy their six-packs of beer or Coke, they see only a thin, young man with bony arms and a crooked nose, a pair of pale blue eyes that look as blank as the white linoleum beneath their feet, hair an indiscernible shade of brown. They never ask him a thing except for the occasional "How you doing today?" or "Good weather we're having, eh?" Jesse is simply ten fingers translating the price of the candy bar into the beige cash register, taking their money, giving them change.

He sits on his stool in the store, reading a tabloid, his cheek smashed into his hand. The day has been excruciatingly slow. It's noon now, only six customers since six a.m. Not that he wishes for more business. He used to dislike the customers—their stained teeth, jagged mustaches, sweat-stained armpits. Now he barely sees them, but he's aware of a dullness in his body after he spends the day taking cash from those grease-lined hands. If he had to choose, he'd take the boredom; he'd sit beneath the ticking wall clock and let the day slide past, uninterrupted.

But this never happens. The bell fastened to the door clangs. Jesse looks at the woman walking toward him and doesn't mutter the obligatory

"Can I help you?" He can't help anyone. If a customer needs to locate the Folgers or the Pepto-Bismal, she'll ask him on her own.

But this woman doesn't go to the shelves; she doesn't ask him anything. She just looks at him, her green eyes fringed with blond lashes. She's obese. Her cheeks float up toward her eyes, ending at the deep indents beneath the sockets. Her hair is streaked with blond and there's a kindness to her face that's almost doll-like. She's got a box propped on one hip, and as Jesse looks at it, he notices her shorts are riding up into the deep crevices between her thighs and crotch. She leans forward, resting her breasts on the counter. Her neckline plunges dangerously low; you could bury an apple in her cleavage.

Jesse sighs. "Can I help you?" he asks, folding the tabloid. She straightens and her breasts climb back onto her body like little animals onto a tree.

"I was hoping so," she says. And then she averts her eyes. She seems to be screwing her courage into place, working herself up to something.

She opens the flaps of the box and rummages through some crumpled newspaper, pulling from it another box. This one's made of white plastic—like an old first-aid kit without the decal. She slides the box across the counter.

"I made them," she says. "I was hoping you'd help me sell them." Jesse unlatches the plastic fastener. Inside the box are dozens of tiny plastic babies with rhinestones in their bellies. They're the size of large houseflies, glued to metal brooch backings and are separated into little compartments according to the color of their stone. Blue with blue, violet with violet, pink with pink. On each compartment, a word is glued. Tranquility, Solitude, Hope, Forgiveness, Mercy... They're just pins, crudely made—he's seen similar things at the stationary store downtown—rocks with words on them, rings with stones that have special meanings. He picks up a Mercy baby and looks at the cool blue ember in its stomach, as if it had eaten a gas flame. He turns it over and can see the lump of glue that attaches it to the pin back. He digs a fingernail into it. It's not hard enamel; his nail sinks in.

The fan above them whirs and the refrigerator case clicks on, a second tier of whirring, and Jesse feels that he can hear the woman's insides spinning, too. She's nervous, her fists balled up beside her and she stands too still, watching him.

"They have special powers," the woman says. "I've been making them for a while now, just for the people I know, and they're working. I know it sounds like crazy talk, but I'm telling you." She leans forward again, her cleavage like the entry into a secret universe. "I'm telling you." She's so close Jesse can smell her perfume—something baby powdery but with a sweeter, more complicated undertone—warm and glandular. There's a slight sheen to her pale skin. In her ears she wears two tiny crosses. One of them is crooked; the flesh around it is slightly pink.

"I'm not really allowed to take consignment stuff," Jesse says finally, pushing the box back to her. "This is a mini-mart." She puts her hand on the box.

"You've had it hard," she says abruptly. Her voice is judgmental but still kind. "If you don't mind me saying, you have the eyes of someone who's known his share of trouble."

The bell clangs again. A teenage boy with shifty, dark eyes.

"Yeah," Jesse says, watching the kid. "Whatever."

"No, I mean it," the woman says. "I can tell. You lost someone. I can see that in people. I know."

Jesse looks back at the woman. This is irritating—as if she is wiggling something tender inside him.

"I can't help you," he says. "This isn't a jewelry store."

"It's not jewelry," the woman says. She takes the blue-bellied Mercy baby that Jesse'd been looking at and sets it on the counter in front of him. "Have this," she says. She repacks her box slowly and then sets it in the larger box, tucking the newspaper around carefully. On her way out the door, she turns to look at him again. She lifts one hand as if to wave, but it looks more like she's shooing away a fly.

The kid buys three bags of chips and a pack of Camels—Jesse never cards—and then the mart is quiet. Jesse unfolds the tabloid again, resting his foot on the low shelf behind the counter.

A few minutes later, the bell clangs again. This time it's Ahn.

"Dude," Ahn says, walking up behind the counter. She heaves herself up and sits on it, inches from Jesse. "The weirdest thing happened this morning." Ahn's usually sallow face is rose with excitement.

"You don't even care, do you?" Ahn asks, chewing on a hangnail. She's got a collection of plastic bracelets that go halfway up her arm and several beaded necklaces around her neck. She must be going through some sort of bohemian phase. When they were in high school, Jesse thought he might sleep with her. She was never pretty, her brown hair too dull, her small eyes too close together, but she'd had a kind of worldliness. Her dad was in jail and she lived with an aunt in a sea of foster kids.

"What," Jesse says. It's more of a statement than a question and Ahn looks him over for a moment before speaking.

"There was another car wreck at Eleventh and Garfield," she says. "A bus wreck, actually."

Jesse's heart seizes up. He looks down at the tabloid for a minute. He's aware of a stillness creeping through his body, as if a thin membrane is drifting over his heart.

Ahn reaches over and pulls a pack of Skittles off the candy shelf near the register and rips it open. Jesse watches as the shiny colored dots collect in her small palm. "That intersection is cursed," she says. Jesse knows it's his turn to talk, but his throat feels full, as if he's swallowed a bone.

"I was biking to work to pick up my check," she continues, "and this bus was totally out of control. The brakes were busted, I guess. This old lady was at the crosswalk with this little dog and the dog just scooted out into the street—he was on one of those leashes that goes out forever—and he just ran right out in front of the bus and instead of the bus just running over it, the driver tried to swerve and went right into another car which spun out and flipped over the curb and wiped out the mailboxes." Ahn threw a handful of candy in her mouth.

The pain in Jesse's throat subsides somewhat.

"Did the dog live?" he asks. He doesn't know why he asks this; he's almost whispering. Ahn doesn't seem to care. She snorts.

"Yeah, ohmigod—the lady picked it up and started screaming. She was like eighty years old. You never see old people scream. It was a total trip. I wanted to stay and watch them clean it up—people probably died—but Jane was only going to be there from noon to one, and I wouldn't have gotten paid till next week."

The Mercy baby sits on the counter next to Ahn. Jesse fixes his attention on the little prism of blue light in its gut. It could almost be pretty if it weren't so weird.

"I'll give you a call later," Jesse says, folding up the tabloid. Ahn swings her dangling legs for a moment, cocks her head and studies him.

"I just thought you'd want to know," she says, slides off the counter, and leaves.

For a while, Jesse just sits, concentrating on the knuckles of his hands. There's a false silence in his body—as if the music were turned up so loud he'd gone deaf.

Three years ago, his girlfriend, Lucy Star-Beckett died at that intersection. She was seventeen. Jesse still keeps a photograph of her in a shoe box in his closet. He barely ever looks at it, but it seems to be the only real image of her face he can manufacture. Lucy Star-Beckett, age seventeen, sitting on a car hood, stoned and glassy-eyed, her black hair in a high, tight ponytail, her face narrow and unsmiling. He'd tried to throw the photograph away after she died, creasing it down the center, burying it underneath tissues in the bathroom. But he'd woken up in the middle of the night and retrieved it. It ended up tucked in a box, out of sight, but still present. Lucy Star-Beckett, age seventeen, blood the cool silver of mercury, a heart that beat irregularly, a smell that never seemed quite human when he lay next to her in his bedroom beneath the old flannel sleeping bag. She smelled like burned nuts and metal, even down between her long, shapeless legs, even down where she should have smelled animal and dank, she smelled like the inside of a gun.

Jesse closes his eyes, tries to stave off a wave of panic, then turns back to the tabloid. His thoughts are not thoughts; they're a hum, a burst of red and terrible static. These are the feelings he tries to avoid. But inside the hum, his resistance is caving. A fist unclenching in his chest, a weird blooming hand in his heart.

They'd been in bed. Lucy's hair was tangled and her mascara smeared. She was a little drunk, a little high, and instead of being calm, languid on the flannel sleeping bed as she usually was, she'd gotten upset. It was something stupid. Something about how Jesse wouldn't look at her when he asked her questions. And in order to stop her from going on he leaned across the bed and kissed her. Hard. He knew she wouldn't want him to. Her lips hardened against her teeth. She collapsed backward onto the quilt and clawed her way out from under his weight. "Knock it off," she yelled, her breath sharp with alcohol, her hair skunked with pot. She kept yelling—words he can't remember—empty, angry words. She seemed temporarily crazy—hyper and mean. And he'd grabbed her by the waistband of her skirt. It tore. It surprised them both and she quieted for a moment. It seemed like she was waiting. It was some sort of challenge. He didn't know what he was going to do—even then, with the skirt torn and his free hand pressing her down onto the bed—he only knew what his hands told him. That he needed her to be quiet, that her anger was severing something he couldn't bear to have severed, that he felt this old pain opening in his chest, that he needed to be close to her. And so he pushed her face-down on the bed, opening her thighs with his knee, not bothering to take her underwear off, just pushing it aside.

And it had hurt him, too, but the release felt like release, despite their chafed skin, despite the way she lay beneath him, soft and limp, not even trying to turn over.

She wouldn't talk to him after it and her silence was a judgment he couldn't tolerate.

Why had he done it? They'd always had tender sex or lusty sex or bored, casual sex—her mouth giving and soft, her forehead fitting nicely into his neck. It had been an aberration. There had only been the want and the roar. And he needed her to understand this implicitly, to forget about it as if it had been a film they'd seen. Dark and disturbing but not in her life.

That was it, and then she was gone. What the connection was between the act that had taken place that evening and the car accident after she left that had flung her body out a windshield and into the careening path of another driver, killing her instantly, was never clear to Jesse. He felt implicated but never charged—an unending, restless feeling. Had she not left his apartment, had she stayed the night as she usually did, getting to class late because they liked to mess around in the morning—had she not been distracted by the pain between her legs, by the thrumming red in her mind as she tried to think—then maybe her reflexes would have been quicker, she would have seen the car coming the wrong way down the road. But she'd been drinking, she'd been high, and she'd been distracted. And they put her down in the ground with her dead mother near the golf course and he never once went to the grave, not even to the funeral, and he never mentioned her, not to anyone, not ever.

His shift lasts until three. Until two o'clock he sips beers and stares at the Mercy baby. Six more customers come in. At two-fifteen, he picks up the baby and unhooks the pin. He pokes his finger until a drop of blood rises to the surface, then feels silly, and rehooks it, slipping the baby into his pocket.

When his shift ends, Jesse gets on his bike and heads west. He's not been up Eleventh Avenue since Lucy's car wreck. If he goes over to this side of town, he uses the smaller streets. But mostly, he just stays away. Nothing is different, he tells himself as the blood thins and races through his limbs, as his heart speeds with the exertion of biking up the hill toward the Avenue. But something is different. His heart feels raw. It's a terrible feeling. A pain in his jaw, his eyes, his chest, his throat. He feels his body gravitating toward Lucy's old neighborhood the way an eye travels to the horror of a wound.

He knows where he's headed but his mind and body are not in sync. It is as though his thoughts have unhooked from the mechanism that gives them tension and are just flapping into space.

He'd never questioned his aversion to this part of the city; it just made sense. He had to live out his days. This was his sentence; this is what separated him and Lucy now.

He reaches Eleventh and Garfield. A donut shop with an orange neon sign, a white apartment complex, a gas station. Nothing is different. And indeed, nothing is different here. What had he expected? A permanent jag of lightning hovering in the sky? A colorful shrine of glass and mirrors reflecting Lucy's face in a thousand permutations?

When he'd first heard about Lucy's accident, it seemed to Jesse that she had done it to punish them—Jesse, her vanished brother, her drunken father. Maybe she'd seen the car swerving the wrong way down the street and saw within that moment the possibility of exit.

The traffic light turns green. Then yellow and then red and two teenage girls stop in a blue hatchback. Jesse stares in the window until one of them looks over and giggles. She turns to say something to the other and he looks away.

Down the street, Jesse sees the spot Ahn had described. Yellow police ropes have cordoned it off. The mailboxes are laying on their sides on the grass across the street. Jesse continues to ride.

He thought he would stop at Lucy's house nearby, but as he nears, his legs act without him, they pedal furiously past it. He doesn't even look at it, though he feels it spitting out a heat. He rides straight down the street for a long time, until it jags into a smaller street, until it turns into the road through a city park.

There isn't much that frightens him. He can sit through horror films with a wry calm, deal with the constant stream of freaks at the mini-mart. But this dark, wooded city park has always disturbed him. It's disorienting. The trees grow where they please; the leaves blanket a floor he can't see. He turns onto a dirt path that runs near the creek.

It's not nature, exactly, this patch of urban forest. He hasn't come to seek peace or commune with the murky creek that cuts through at an angle. Fast-food wrappers float serenely downstream and a shopping cart protrudes from the shallows, wedged in mud. He's there because it's foreign enough, shaded enough, to match the darkness of his mood.

No one ever associated Jesse with Lucy's death. No one would have thought of it. She was scraped off the pavement and put in a box and with her went the details of everything she had lived through. And it would have been crazy to go around confessing—especially since he didn't mean it that way; he was only trying to settle something important inside himself.

Two nights before she died she called Jesse and asked him to come over. "The house is too quiet," she said. "If you come over I'll make you dinner." And so he'd come, picking a loaf of bread out of the bread dumpster behind the bakery. She'd already cooked the noodles and was heating the sauce when he came in. She smiled, her eyes deadened, as they always were. And he had barely set down the bread when her father, Peter, came stumbling in through the back door, holding a vodka bottle. Lucy froze, her hand on the wooden spoon, and Peter came up behind her. He stood with his body pressed against her back. Jesse felt cemented in place, as if something awful were about to occur. But Peter just nestled his pallid face in Lucy's hair and drilled a kiss into the back of her head. That's all that happened. Peter kissed her head for so long that Lucy finally turned her gaze from the sauce to Jesse, her eyes frightened, pleading. And then Peter lifted his head, inhaled the smell of her dark hair, and stumbled off to the bathroom.

Jesse stood watching and Lucy turned off the stove. She went to the sink and for a moment Jesse thought she was going to cry. But she simply washed her hands, put them on the edge of the sink, then turned to face him.

"Come here for a second," she said.

In her bedroom, she took her pipe out from the little ceramic box by her bed. Jesse never liked the way pot made him feel, but he had no objections to her habit. He watched her hand hovering over the bowl like a moth, lighting it. Silver smoke twined from her mouth and nose. Her lids grew velvety. She put the pipe away.

And then, she unbuttoned her shirt.

Jesse didn't want this. She unhooked her bra. Undid the buttons of her jeans. Rolled down her underwear.

He really didn't want this. The kiss in the kitchen had made him feel strange, as if the hollowness that blew through this house might win, might take all of them with it. He wanted to touch her, but fully clothed, something clean and safe.

Jesse stood with his back against the wall and didn't move. She approached, her body hard, thin. She put her face up to his.

"Please Jesse," she said, and took his hand.

He couldn't move. If he touched her the way she was asking him to, he was afraid he would collapse. It felt untrue. Though he often felt he might love her, in this moment the intimacy felt grim; if he let his body sink into hers now it would melt with that kiss. It would be merely an extension of that sadness.

She trembled; the room was cold. Her hands were at his crotch. Deft fingers, always quick at unbuttoning, unzipping.

She knelt.

Jesse let his weight drop back against the wall, his pants halfway down his thighs. Lucy's tongue worked furiously; he was soft. He felt the wet pull and release. Her cool fingers startled his balls. And he gave over to it, though he didn't want to, though it still felt wrong. He was ice in the glare of the sun; nature was against him.

Her eyes stayed shut. He got hard. He looked down and could see that all her muscles were taut. Even the tiny knobs on the tops of her shoulders seemed rigid with purpose.

And as the sensations traveled through his body—that seductive mix of warmth and light—so did a feeling of shame.

He didn't touch her until the moment the heat reached its peak and pooled all through his body, rising as if he had turned to liquid, as if he were about to go shooting out of his skin. Then he grabbed her by the hair and yanked her away.

And it was as he feared. With her hair gripped firmly in his hand, Jesse felt a wave of grief so strong it nearly parted him straight down his core.

The woods have the quality of a padded room. Jesse sits on the muddy bank of the creek and water quickly seeps through his pants. He takes off his shoes and throws them up the incline near his bike. He considers taking off all his clothes, walking into the creek. But he knows better.

He leans back, aware as he does this that his shirt is getting wet and muddy. He's barely visible to the world now, huddled here on the bank. The only real clue to his presence is his bike, stashed by the tree above.

Something sharp pokes his tailbone and Jesse reaches behind him. A small, white, child's teacup with a tiny red rose on one side. The handle is broken and it's covered in mud. Jesse wipes it off on his shirt and stares at it. He traces the rim of the small cup with his finger.

Jesse reaches in his pocket for the Mercy baby. The thin thing has moved from his heart and floats listlessly through his body. And as he takes the baby from his pocket, he notices the blue stone in its belly has come loose, has fallen out of his pocket, and is lost.

FLUENCY

AT A DINNER PARTY, SEVERAL MONTHS AGO, ONE OF EVAN'S friends from work asked me to tell her the moment I knew "that Evan was the one for me." I hate questions like these. They always make me feel small-hearted. I loved him. But there was no moment. There was no blinding flash.

"I'll tell you in a second," I said, hoping she'd be swept into another conversation while I went to the bathroom. When I came back, she was talking animatedly with Evan's newly divorced friend. In bed later, I looked at Evan's body, heavy with alcohol and sleep. His dark hair was very thick, curlier at his temples. His lips got a shade pinker with drink. I even knew his breath. You could snap your fingers in the gap between his inhale and his exhale. And as I inventoried these things I knew about him, a softness fell into me. Is this what Evan's friend wanted me to tell her? Was this softness the synonym of love?

During the first six months that we dated, I was plagued with terrible dreams. My teeth would turn to blue cheese in my mouth. My mother would come back to life in a blissful flash, only to die again because I couldn't get a pill out of a jar in time. I woke up emitting strangled sounds, my T-shirts drenched with sweat, my face either pale with lack of blood or flushed with too much of it. The first time Evan slept over, I startled awake from a dream in which I was stuck beneath the ice of a lake. Evan sat, his spine rigid. There was no trace of dream in his buggy blue eyes. He coiled a long arm around me and I could feel the steady thumping of his heart against my cheek. It seemed so safe in there, inside the parlor of his rib cage. He never asked me what was wrong or if I was okay. In the morning, when we were drinking our coffee, he simply put his hand between my shoulder blades.

I lost my mother when I was ten. Evan's died in childbirth. His father and my father died the same year, when we were sophomores in college.

The fall I met Evan—the fall of our failing fathers—we were in the dean's office waiting to fill out paperwork in order to take the rest of the semester off. Evan—whose name I did not yet know—stood glumly, leaning on the counter, his dark hair glossy under the florescent lights. He toyed with the little leather strap of his watchband and shifted his weight from side to side. The receptionist, a glamorous blond with a limp, must have been new. She was all alone in that big room and couldn't find anything. She knelt and fooled with a box of paper under the counter. In my head, I was making a list of things I would have to figure out: which rabbi to call, how to sell my father's piano, how to deal with the savings bonds I knew he would leave me.

"Jesus Christ, my father will be dead before this woman finds her forms," Evan said. I looked up into his pale, thin face and said, "My dad's dying, too."

Ten years have passed since then. It's impossible to believe. And there is no suitable answer to the question Evan's friend asked. I married Evan because he had no one else. His parents had died; he had no siblings, no tangled mess of cousins, uncles, aunts. He married me for the same reason. In this arrangement, we both secured something. We could guard against the possibility of floating endlessly outward, alone, in a sea without islands or rocks. And all these years this decision has made sense to us. No—the decision has turned into a love so complicated I can't tell Evan's colleague about it because it wouldn't match her version.

When I was a kid at summer camp, we played many games that required dying. There was the game in which one camper murdered other campers by winking, and the detective had to figure out who the winker/killer was.

Or, when the counselors were at the lodge, one of the campers, Stacy Marvel, would do her "one minute of death" trick. I would never play, though I remember watching with a certain amount of curiosity, the line of pony-tailed girls in their T-shirts and sweatpants, one by one holding their breath as Stacy came from behind and knocked the wind out of them. They'd gather around. "What did you see?" they'd ask as the fallen girl's face melted back to life beneath the glare of the battery lantern. And each girl would describe the thing she was supposed to: a dark tunnel with a flickering light in the distance. Or, if the girl were especially creative, she might see a blue globe like a Japanese anchor filled with fireflies, or—my favorite: a glowing man with his hands on fire, beckoning.

I sat on the edge of my bunk bed, eleven years old one summer, twelve the next, and watched. The girls thought I was chicken—they rolled their eyes when I continued, night after night, to sit the game out. But really I just knew too well that they were lying. I knew that what you saw when you got the wind knocked out of you was blackness, that it didn't compare to the busyness of death. In your body when you're dying, my mother told me, there is a lot of talking. It gets stranger and stranger, she said, the talking, until you seem to know another language. And when you are fluent, you have to leave.

There are so many languages to learn. It would be a different world if people recognized this. If, instead of listing Spanish or French on the "languages" section of an application, you could write what you really know. All the various ways to be silent about things. Death. Betrayal. The way that certain kinds of language can lead you away from those bottomless pits of loss and the way that other kinds of language can show you the bottoms of them.

Evan did not ask about my nightmares because he knew there was no way to talk about them that would transmit the thing from me to him. To reduce the images to words would have been futile. It's a joke, this kind of talking—and since the moment he put his hand between my shoulder blades I knew he knew this. I understood that he would have sat cross-legged on my bunk with me, in a curious silence, never trying to tell those pink-cheeked girls that they were wrong.

Shortly after we got married, Evan was sideswiped in a terrible car wreck. Our small Honda was crushed but Evan was almost unscathed. He had bruises where the seatbelt held him and a strange scratch on his cheek. But all his bones were unbroken, all his organs whole. They let him come home from the hospital that same day, releasing him with a band-aid and a gruff pat on the back. No one told us that Evan would catch the nightmares from this, that he would wake up yelling, grabbing onto the headboard. The first night it happened, his eyes were full of sirens. He began to whimper, his body bracketing my own. Alison, he said after his fear had ebbed, thank you for marrying me. I said nothing; I just put my hand between his shoulder blades.

You can't ask for this sort of fluency. No. You either bang against this thing by chance or you sail right past it.

We wake just as we have every Saturday for years. Evan's cheek is creased from the crumpled pillowcase. He's on his side, staring bleary-eyed at our terrible vine wallpaper, quilt tangled between his long legs. I stumble to the bathroom, to the kitchen to make coffee. He follows later, takes sections of the paper, scatters them around him on the couch in the living room.

When we were first married, we could sit like that all day, reading one another bad headlines, making ourselves sick with too much coffee. But there is a quiet that has settled into even this small act. Evan sets aside the front section and the calendar for me. He settles into the cushions, his white shirt soft against the cream upholstery. He still sits the same way he used to sit when we were twenty-two, with one knee tucked beneath his chin, the paper under his foot. We talk about the garden. We talk about groceries. But mostly we just sit with the sun on our necks as we read.

This morning, though, I want to talk about the summer. We've been planning a vacation for months. Or, I have.

"So, Ev," I say. "What if we waited until July?" I do this gently. He's been hesitant about money. I would like to go to Spain. But I'd settle for Mexico. Even New Mexico. His eyes are trained on the wood floor; it looks as if he might peel the planks up with the force of his gaze.

I know this man. I have lived with him through the only years that seem to matter now. But this expression is new. There are locks in his eyes, in the muscle of his jaw. Before my mind can register fear, my heart begins to beat faster. I feel a chill and settle beside him on the couch.

"What's the matter?" I ask. The question flies from its cage and clings to him. I'm immediately sorry I asked. He looks like he might be sick. Maybe I don't want to know.

"Alison," he says. It's a new, grave way to say my name. The heaviness to it, the emptiness of those three soft syllables. "I think I need to be alone for a while."

"Alone," I repeat. It could almost be a name he wants me to call him. I think I need to be Alone for a while, Evan isn't doing it for me. My mind goes blank. And then, I imagine that I can leave him for the day. I can go to the hardware store, buy some bulbs for the yard. He could go on a walk. Have dinner at the beach by himself.

"Okay." And then, a moment of doubt. "What kind of alone?"

"Alone," he says again, louder, and turns his face toward me. Is it possible, in seven years of being together, we have never uttered this word?

"I think I should move out."

In my body, all motion halts. My heart, my blood, my thoughts. Even my eyes seem to freeze on the image of the living room, still as a photograph: the paper on the coffee table, the rings of coffee staining the text, the chairs with no one sitting in them, Evan beside me, a frozen man.

And then a violence creeps across my limbs. I want to smack him across the face, send his head cracking against the plaster of the wall. There's no way to undo this. He can't possibly want it.

Shut up, I want to yell. Don't be such an idiot.

Neither of us say anything for a minute. And then I say, "You can't."

My words are toy soldiers guarding a very real country. The only feeling in my body is one of ice. If I don't move at all, will things stop progressing? Will it not get any worse?

We sit in silence. He puts his hand on mine. It could be any organ of his body, cooled and exhumed, come to rest on my clenched fist.

"I'm not happy," he continues. "I don't know why. I can't figure it out. I'm just not. Happy."

I listen to his words fall into their ordinary slots of meaning. I (noun) am (verb) not (modifier) happy (adjective). Yes. The miracle of the sentence. Not happy. How can I fail to understand?

"I don't understand," I whisper. I sound odd, even to myself. The whisper comes out sounding like a tire being stabbed. I don't understand.

There are so many things I've never told him. Not the things I can't say. Just small things. Things I suddenly wish he knew. Like, when I was younger, I used to imagine that there was a world parallel to this world where all lost things went to wait. If I lost the gold ring, it was waiting for me in that other world. So was the hairbrush, the stuffed zebra, my mother's amethyst earring, my mother's solid brass spoon, my mother.

He doesn't know about this world or what place he will take in it.

He doesn't know that my disdain for pretzels stems from those awful nights in the hospital waiting room, the vending machine busted, the nurses handing out small bags of these dry salty twigs.

He doesn't know that the tiny scar at the base of my hairline is from the incision of a doctor's knife to take out a mole.

He doesn't know that he cannot leave. That this is an impossibility akin to changing the world or eating cement.

I feel my heart dropping down low, dangling by too fine a thread, and I think of arguing. He was happy last weekend—we went to the beach. The wind made his hair puffy and his windbreaker smack against itself. He picked up a whole sand dollar and we held hands as the waves drenched our shoes. Or if not last weekend, we could just take two nights ago. I made him pasta and mustard greens and held his toe while we watched the news. He put a sleepy hand on my neck. Weren't these the gestures of happy? I could make a pretty good case. But even as the phrases arrange themselves in my mind, I know I've lost. A numbness winds through my body—a survival mechanism protecting me from the crushing weight to follow. It wouldn't matter what I said, his words would always be there.

"I'm sorry, Alison," he says. Sorry! I want to scream it at him. Heat streaks through my muscles. What does it mean? You can be sorry you have to cancel dinner plans or sorry you stepped on a person's foot but can you really be sorry for quietly exiting a marriage?

There's nothing to say to this; I am still upholding the rule we've agreed on all these years. It won't be me who transgresses. But the silence has lost its tact. I can feel it hardening inside of my chest. Becoming something darker.

I shake his cold hand off my own and walk to the bathroom.

I was young when my mother died. But in some ways, I think I might have had a better understanding of loss. I didn't try to bargain with it. I simply invented ways of living next to it. I talked to my mother by whispering into the whorls on trees in the yard. The branches shaking in the wind were my confirmation that she had heard me. And when Mary Owen told me that this was stupid, I began to do inventory on my body. One two three four five fingers on a hand. Twelve thirteen fourteen teeth upstairs in my mouth.

There's no pain in my body, just the beginning of a loud, terrible buzzing.

I stand and turn on the sink to drown it out. My reflection in the medicine cabinet balks back at me. Quickly, I open the door. Rows of pills, tweezers, soaps, and toners are lined up. A box of Q-tips. A cup full of makeup. Ordinarily, these things would give me comfort. The colorful, pointless emblems of survival.

I pick up Evan's tube of natural shaving cream. It's crushed in the center, bent helplessly over itself. My pulse quickens with anger. The same hand from my brain that stopped me from hitting Evan grabs hold of my heart.

All of these years, Evan's presence has been a kind of antidote to silence. Those pieces of his daily life that are littered across the bathroom—his silver razor in its blue box, his bay rum soap, the fancy haircutting scissors—have been a comfort to me. I was given his life instead of the others. In a way, he took the place of that old oak tree in my childhood yard. I no longer needed to whisper into the dark little warped spots on branches. Instead, I could feel the heat of his body next to mine on the couch, smell the animal burn of his hair. With his solid mass of bones and muscle in my life, all our losses were wordlessly contained.

But maybe I misinterpreted the language we shared. Maybe I wrote into his silence half of a dialogue in which he was not complicit.

I put the shaving cream back in the cabinet and run my fingers over the various bottles and jars. There is something different in the air around me. Maybe it isn't dust. It may be the residue of his words making the air thicker, more difficult to breathe. Or it may be something inside me, not in the air at all. There had been something secret in the cells of my mother, in the heart of my father, and now somewhere vague in Evan. A language that each of them alone had learned without me. And who's to say what the first words of this new language were? A lump in the breast, a strange pain in the chest, a buzzing in the ears.

I take the box of Q-tips out and grab a fistful. They are slender and vulnerable, like tiny fainted women in my hand. I begin to break them over the sink, one by one.

There had been a girl at summer camp—a limp, frail blond, who had not come easily back into the world when she passed out during the dying game. The girls tried everything, singing, yelling, slapping her face, stroking her hair. But nothing fazed her. Eventually the counselor was called back from the lodge, the nurse came with her, and the girl was carried off. She went home after that, and all the girls talked about it. Was she faking it? Was she dead during those strange minutes? And if so, what did she see with so much more time to see it? In my head, she is the hero of the game. She is its only authentic player.

HOLISM

"WOULD YOU STILL LOVE ME IF I ONLY HAD ONE ARM?" MICHAEL asks. He's not looking at Ella. Even in the dark she can tell he's gazing fixedly toward the ceiling.

"I would, I think," she says.

"What if I only had fingers and no arms?"

Ella considers this.

"That would be difficult," she says. It's late, so late. The birds are beginning to chirp though it's still dark out.

"It would be difficult to love me or difficult to have only fingers?"

"Oh, Michael," she says. He waits. "Both, I guess."

"Then you're a shallow lover." They've been through this sort of thing before. Ella sighs.

"Would you love me if I didn't have my nose?" she asks.

"Your nose or any nose?"

"Any nose."

"Of course I'd still love you," he says.

The night her nose disappears she realizes that the sight of her shocks him. "Your nose!" he manages, though his voice sounds faint and very far away. "Oh, Ella..." He reaches for her, as if to hold her, but when she fails to crumble quiet and broken into his arms, he recoils.

"I can see everything you're thinking," he says to her that night as they lie in bed, their skin lit by streetlights. "I can tell you are thinking unfaithful thoughts."

Ella imagines Michael peering through her as if she were a viewfinder, looking at her thoughts projected on a tiny screen tacked to the back of her skull. Ella and her old lovers flashing like a string of glittering rhinestones, gaudy and intense. Syrupy words and promises leaping and fading. Or a little chart of her passions, Michael scoring lower than the strong taste of cheese or the way it feels to drag a razor across the stubble of her thigh. And what if he could see her dreams?

She suddenly feels exposed—as if her body has secrets to be ashamed of.

"I am not," she tells him.

The hole in her head is as smooth as her pink gums. She touches her ring finger to the rim of the cavity.

"It's changed everything, Ella," he tells her. "It's revealed you for what you are."

In this moment, a feeling of shame knits with indignation and hangs there inside Ella like a knot.

He gets up from the bed. His body is thin. In the dim light of the bedroom she can see the hollow beneath his ribs, his chest hair patchy and coiled. She keeps her finger on the slick skin around the hole. There is a great deal of sensation there. Touching it sends a dull thrilling pain through her.

He dresses in the darkness, fumbles for his shoes. She doesn't try to stop him. She imagines what he'll tell his sisters. "She was unfaithful," he'll sob, and they'll purse their lips and stroke his dark hair. "I saw it with my own eyes." With this, the sisters will sigh like they're extinguishing an era. "Well, good riddance," the oldest one will say. "The pretty ones are always deceitful."

She can hear him walk down the hallway, out the door, down the stairs of the apartment. The night outside is wet and cold. His headlights go on, flash the walls. The world becomes light and shadow.

She might have married him! she thinks. People lose more than noses in life, after all. What good would his promises have been?

In the morning, she wakes up curious. Light dusts through the curtains. She feels an unfamiliar heaviness in her limbs and it takes her several attempts to rise from bed. When she does, she sees her reflection in the mirror and starts.

She studies it. A soft purple skin has formed around the hole. It's delicate, almost transparent. At first, she imagines what Michael must have seen. Her smooth face, wide eyes, twiggy neck, all orbiting this new feature. Or featurelessness. She supposes it would be difficult to see anything else; the vacancy is so pronounced, so obvious. It's a clean-looking hole, though, framed nicely by the scar. Ella turns to see her profile and realizes that she looks rather stunning without the distraction of that sharp feature; the oddity catches the eye. A smoothness and unity to the face that wasn't present before.

This sets her apart from the world. Humans are supposed to have noses. But she finds this separation somewhat tantalizing. People place so much value on the things they take for granted. She imagines Michael having parties for his fingers, his eyes. How grateful he must feel when he gets out of the shower, his nose a sturdy triangular protrusion, a working set of tunnels, a sign of normalcy and all it implies.

Ella is reminded of a time when she and Michael went to the funeral of one of his sisters' babies. The sister, Margaret, was clutching a napkin the entire afternoon, her fingers white with tension. She heaved and sobbed and grew frightfully silent, but all the while there was this strange power brewing inside her. She became wounded and regal, gifted with a sad yet powerful magnetism.

In the kitchen, over a cup of coffee, Ella realizes that her life will quickly become defined by the thing she is missing.

Ella takes the elevator down to shop for fruit. The city whirs by, overcoats and black bags and the smell of overlapping perfume and car exhaust. She stops beneath the awning of the grocery. Over the bin of oranges, a woman meets her eyes as if to ask her something and then quickly looks away. Ella raises her hand from the bin to stroke her warm new place but stops abruptly. She looks around, sees many eyes diverting.

A young man with dark hair gets into a blue pickup truck across the street. "Michael," she begins but falters when her voice emerges sounding like a bleat.

She pauses to see if anyone has noticed but all the people at the grocery are pretending not to see her. She squints in the direction of the truck and sees that the man looks nothing like Michael. What might the real Michael be doing now in this city without her? She imagines him sipping coffee distractedly. Circling passages in books that relate to his life.

For a moment, she feels her heart tugging backward inside her, longing for a place it used to rest. Michael—that familiar body, the pools of heat he left on her sheets. She winces, tries to still the sensation. She straightens her spine, swipes at her long hair with a clawed hand. The skin around the hole is more sensitive than her other skin and she can feel each tiny breath of the city—each passing car and cough, each clean breeze whisking by.

"Excuse me," a man says as he brushes past Ella on his way to the street. He holds his eyebrows high and arches away from her as if she is made of thorns. Ella bristles; if she had thorns she'd stick one right into this man's balding scalp.

All these ridiculous people, she thinks. Waking, dressing, working, sleeping, dreaming dreams that they won't remember. Ella's indignation rises.

As she walks back to her apartment, oranges in hand, she pauses to look at some paper that has escaped from the overflowing trash can. It brushes and spins over the pavement. For a moment, Ella feels herself spiraling, too, coat and scarf trailing behind her, heaved up like leaves in the crisp fall wind.

Months pass and deep into winter, snow hiding the dirt and garbage of the city streets, the phone rings in her apartment.

"I'm sorry," Michael says. He sounds windless and drunk.

She is quiet on the other end. Her fingers snake into the hole.

"Ella. Ella, are you there?" She waits. His breathing is labored and raspy. "Ella, I know you're there. I've done a lot of thinking and—"

She hears a clattering on the other end of the line. Some voices. Then a click of a door and relative quiet. He seems to falter. She remains silent.

"So how are you?"

She considers rolling her eyes at this, but she's alone and the effect would be lost. She tilts her head and loops a lock of blond hair around her index finger.

He clears his throat.

"Anyway, Ella, I've been thinking it would be nice to see each other."

She considers this and yanks on the hair. It is solidly rooted to her scalp.

"Maybe meet up for dinner one night."

"Fine." Her voice has become tinny and smeared as a result of the hole. She is conscious that he takes note of this.

"I have been reading about your condition, Ella," he says to her after they are seated beneath a wrought-iron lamp studded with blobs of red glass. She raises her eyebrows. "I mean, I don't want to overstep but I just think this is something that if you really tried, you could fix."

She notices that he has begun to grow a little beard. It seems so deliberate, hanging off his chin in a little point, drawing the eye away from his forehead. She stares at his forehead to see if he notices.

The waitress approaches and sets two menus in front of Michael. She doesn't look at Ella. "We're out of the veal," she says, swiveling on her hard little heel, retreating toward the kitchen.

A long silence ensues. Ella studies each item on the menu. Linguini, swordfish, steak, braised quail.

He folds his menu and places it on the table, his hands on top of it.

"Ella," he says, his voice level as if talking to a child. She puts down her menu with a slap.

"What?" Her voice, again, sounds smeared to her. She studies him for grimaces.

"Are you going to try to fix it or not?"

Ella raises her hand toward the hole and tries to remember what life was like before. It shames her slightly that she can't. Michael's eyes are wide and serious. "I suppose I could try," she says.

He picks her up in his truck, a box of spades and plastic bags sit between them in the cab. The snow has given way to a gray wetness, the gutters ripe with dirty streams of melted slush and candy wrappers. They drive through the city to the highway, over the highway to the hills. He parks by a large whirring power plant. The lights blink mutely into the daylight. A light rain is falling.

She doesn't know why he thinks this will work. But she recognizes that he is on some sort of kick and finds the whole thing a little amusing. He read about it, he explained to her, in some kind of journal. And he's certain they will find the nose there.

A dirt path winds up the incline of the hill. They follow the path to a clearing. Ella hasn't seen a meadow like this since she was a child. Lush and green, surrounded by trees. Small holes scatter the landscape. It looks to her like the work of an indecisive gopher.

He hands her a shovel. They get down on their hands and knees and begin to dig. He goes through each lump of dirt as if looking for diamonds. She is less enthusiastic, digging gingerly, patting the lumps with her spade.

They do this for hours. The sun moves across the sky and dusk begins to settle. Finally he stands, looking defeated. A feeling of fear overtakes her. She hadn't thought this ridiculous plan would work but now she is faced with the reality that it hasn't.

They wipe the dirt off the shovels with a rag and place them back in the box. On the path, on the way back to the car, Ella notices a strange mushroom growing from a stump. She leans over to look at it, pokes it with her finger.

"Michael!" she gasps. "I found it!"

Under the naked lightbulb in her bathroom, they discuss how best to reaffix it. It no longer fits elegantly into the space it left behind. Time has wrinkled it, turned it a dirty yellow.

"What if we soak it to rehydrate it?" Michael says, looking closely at the nose which they have placed on a dinner plate in the sink. Ella shrugs.

"Do you think if we sewed it back on it would eventually return to normal?" he asks. Ella wrinkles the spot where her nose once was. The feeling is strange, as if a tight new skin has grown there. It tingles and sends sparks down her legs.

"Maybe we don't have to sew it," he muses. "Maybe we can superglue it."

Ella looks at the nose, still and hard. It casts a tiny shadow on the plate.

A terrible thought dawns on her.

"Maybe this isn't my nose," she says. "Maybe I found someone else's nose." The thought takes on a life of its own, sliding quickly through her. "It really doesn't look like my nose."

"Of course it does. Look," he points to the bent tip. "See the freckles?"

"That's dirt."

"No. Those are freckles. Your freckles."

A twin is said to have pain when the other is in pain. The mind recognizes something in the other body that it recognizes as its own. She stares at the nose and feels nothing.

"I don't think it's my nose."

Michael looks exasperated and stiffens. "Whose nose is it then?"

"I don't know, Michael," she says, her voice rising, smearing. "I'm not claiming to be an expert, but this is not my nose. I would know if it was."

"You knew when you found it."

"No, I didn't." Suddenly the nose looks frightening to Ella. A shriveled, severed part of another person, there in the bright, revealing light of her blue bathroom.

"It is your nose," Michael's brow furrows and he grabs the nose between his thumb and forefinger, thrusting it at her. "IT IS YOUR NOSE!" he yells. She jumps backward and hits her head on the towel hook. Her eyes widen.

"SAY IT!" His voice cracks and for a moment she thinks he's going to cry. The nose looks like a piece of a dog bone, a chewed plastic toy. Ella tries to say something but the words get caught in her throat. She covers the hole on her face with her hand.

"Stop," she whispers.

He lunges at her and pushes her hand away. With his other hand he mashes the shriveled nose against her face until it fits within the hole. It sticks inside, but unkindly. Ella gasps with pain. Blood trickles over her lip.

Over his trembling shoulder, she can see herself in the mirror. The nose juts out at an angry angle, leaving wide spaces on either side of it. She feels the sharpness digging in, the hard edges of the dried nose tearing at the satiny skin.

Michael's shaking increases.

"Don't you want this?" he asks. His hands quiver like fireflies at her cheeks.

She wipes the blood from her lip and shakes her head. "It's not mine, Michael," she says, meeting his eyes.

TERRIBLE
STORY

W ANT CAN MAKE YOU MISERABLE," MY MOTHER SAYS, SHAKING her head. "It's a terrible thing."

I've been trying to finish writing a story. I want so much from it and this is what we've been discussing—that big, murky darkness between what you have and what you would have, if.

"The story is actually about want," I tell her. She doesn't say anything. "So, I guess it's a terrible story." My mother wipes down the counter and arranges some metal trays on top of the toaster. The sun is pooling up in the porcelain sink, bouncing off the faucet, hitting her wedding ring which makes a strange white oval on the ceiling.

"Is it a love story?" my mother asks. I'm sitting at the table, paging through the beginning, a pen dangling from my hand.

"No. It's about kidnapping."

My mother doesn't say anything. She's unwrapping the fish from the butcher paper, readying it for the buttered dish.

"A woman wants a baby, so she gets one."

"She's mentally ill." My mother says this as if she's just decided. It's her particular blend of question and statement. I've never been sure how to respond to this tone.

"No, she's not ill," I say. "She just really wants the baby she kidnaps. That particular baby. No other baby will do."

"Hmmm," she says, slapping the fillet down. "I see."

By the way she says "I see" it's clear that she doesn't see, that she doesn't like the fact that this woman would want something that my mother herself wouldn't want.

"I don't know why you always want to write such mean things when there are so many mean things already in the world." She doesn't look at me when she says this; she looks at the fish. The television is on, as usual, blaring from the living room. Because she's not looking at me when she talks, I decide she's talking to the fish. She doesn't seem to expect a response and the fish stays absolutely still in the buttered dish. It's head-less, tailless, skinless. And she has the nerve to talk about mean things.

But her want isn't mean. It's just a fact. The woman, Ava, the one who kidnaps the baby, is finishing a bagel at a café near the university. Next to her, a woman arrives carrying a baby in a blue snuggly but Ava barely sees her. She sees the baby. He's facing out into the world, hands flopping help-lessly, blue eyes lazy, squinting from the sun. She can't look away.

Some people talk this way about love. They say there is a moment; it lands inside you—this awareness, like nothing you have ever known. The world changes pitch. The trees become welcoming; instead of feeling big and empty, the sky seems a symbol of the hugeness of potential; your body feels more capable than it ever has. Ava has known degrees of this. She has felt a vine of some intoxicating berry wind around her heart. She has had a hard time focusing on her reading. But nothing like this want. A sharp blade cuts through her. Suddenly she is alone in the world with nothing at all save that baby.

The mother is saying that she needs to find a nanny. She needs help. No one told her it would be like this—so overwhelming! And that's when it comes together. Ava leans over and says she couldn't help but overhear—

She is not a criminal in the stereotypical sense of the word. She has no history of drug use, nor is she poor or at the end of her rope. She's an aspir-ing Ph.D. in philosophy who comes from a sturdy middle-class community outside Philadelphia. She's pretty, with dark, shiny hair and honest green eyes. Her manner is upright (this has to do with years of dance lessons) and her speech impeccable, a sign of class and breeding to the mother (who would never say this in such obvious terms, but thinks it all the same).

Katherine, the mother, meets with Ava the same week. They discuss current events and schedules and diaper changing and Katherine feels bathed in relief. She has found this impeccable girl, this smart, engaging girl to nanny her child. It's her only child and she can't imagine taking any chances.

And so Ava enters the lives of Katherine and the baby. The father is alive and well but, Katherine tells her, he is some sort of journalist and is never at home. She shows her a photograph of him in a thick silver frame. Ava studies the picture to see if the baby resembles the father. He doesn't. His anonymity pleases her.

It goes as planned. Ava comes three days a week. A month passes. The baby learns to hold onto things. To focus his gaze and put meaning in it.

The night Ava finally does it, it's raining. A slight mist over the hills. The key slips into the lock. Her hands slip beneath his tiny body. The baby wakes immediately (a bad omen, she thinks) and Ava is fortunate to be in the car, driving away, when he finally opens his face to howl.

You might think she is wracked with guilt, simply bent over with it, a little crazed, at least high on adrenaline. But she's none of these things. In fact, she's calm. She's lived a very different life from mine, full of needs she doesn't hesitate to fulfill, full of desires she has sated. This probably contributes to the trustworthy look on her face. She seems a woman without wants. A woman not prone to fits of desperation or rashness.

My face is not quite so trustworthy. I am constantly looking around me, noticing the imperfections of things and wishing, very acutely, that these things were perfect, or at least less imperfect. I dislike a lot of people. I hate meaningless conversation and my eyes often slam shut with a dark, impenetrable boredom.

If I were the nanny, rather than our good, sweet, sated-looking Ava, I would be a suspect in the baby's abduction. However, I'm so used to wanting things I can't have, I would never steal the child in the first place.

At this point, my mother comments on the terrible motivations of my characters. They always have some dark, indescribable weakness that leads them to sin. (She doesn't actually say "sin" though that's what she means. She says "troubling behavior.") The fish is baking away as she says this, its elastic, muscular flesh turning flaky in the heat.

I think about sin; I think about Ava.

Her parents shed their Catholicism like snakes shed skin. They rarely spoke of God and when they did a chill descended. Ava, as a result, was not able to identify feelings of guilt and in its place felt a reactionary kind of sexiness. As if in order to keep the enigma of guilt at bay she had to have her pleasures spread before her on a bed of soft, dark leather.

Which reminds me of her lover who leaves her. He's not terribly important; he lives in another city, attending classes at a larger university. He has no role in the baby's abduction. But his absence plays a role in how she feels the night of the kidnapping.

He tasted of nothing, this lover of hers. And this quality was so unique that for a while she felt terrified of losing him. It was a quality she could never replace. She was used to men tasting like something—mushrooms dipped in bleach or old, pungent onions. But his body tasted only mildly of salt. This, more than his perfect brow, perfect forearms, cemented him in her heart.

And the night she plans to kidnap the baby, he leaves a message on her voice mail stating that he's sorry he can't tell this to her in person, but he needs to be honest, he met someone else and there's really nothing to say.

He wishes her good luck on her thesis.

She might have been heartbroken by this except that she's so engrossed in the details of her plan to kidnap the baby. If you are hatching something, a plan, a story—the other emotional matters in your life don't have the same sort of resonance. And though Ava got more pleasure from this smell-less lover than any other she had slept with (and there had been a considerable number), she feels him dim and darken quickly in her heart. The want of the baby sharpens, overtakes the want she feels for her lover, and so she feels this want doubly.

Now my mother heaves a giant sigh. The fish is cooked. She shakes her head.

"Obviously," she says, "it isn't true that all want is the same. The nanny wanted the lover. She covets the child. One is normal. One is wrong."

"Coveting makes a better story," I say, beginning to serve myself some salad. My father cuts a piece of fish and glances out the window in a hopeful way, as if there might be a magic carpet flying by. He sees nothing and slips into a silent disappointment.

"I just read a nice love story," my mother says. Her tone is suggestive. "It was historical," she continues. "It took place during a war. It was a very lovely story—"

Just then there is a loud crash outside the window. We jump. My father stands stiffly and looks outside.

"What was that?" my mother asks, setting down her fork and knife. She looks at my father as though it's his fault, whatever it is that just happened out there, where he was looking moments before.

"I'm not sure," he says to the window. His breath fogs little ovals on the glass and I imagine that he is a cartoon man and those fogs are his dialogue bubbles. I get up and look out the window. I don't see anything either.

"Strange," I say. A shock of intrigue pulses through me; I feel a little bit excited by the possibility of tragic drama right outside the door. I want to ask my mother if she feels it, too, this pang of curiosity, as if the world has been lifted up a level. But her face is still full of blame and aimed at my father who is shuffling around for his coat and heading out the door.

He leaves the house and my mother folds her napkin into a triangle, creasing each crease several times with the side of her hand. When he doesn't return right away, my mother and I go outside to see what has happened.

At this point in the story, things get confusing. My mother's forgotten about the nanny, about her bad behavior, about my telling of it, about what this must say about me. Now she's focused on what's occurring in her own life, in the quiet cul-de-sac where she and my father have lived for thirty years.

Outside, it has recently rained. The pavement has a clean, mineral smell, but it's laced with a bit of panic. On the pavement, the neighbor's dog is lying in a pool of blood. The neighbor's seventeen-year-old son is trembling and gesturing to my father whose hands are shoved into his beige raincoat.

If this scene were occurring in my story rather than in my own life, it would be pregnant with possibilities. Maybe the dog would symbolize something lost in the familial relationship. Maybe it would be a portent of sorts—the little reminder that life is fleeting.

In fiction, often these things are the catalyst for the real dramatic moment. The family is stagnant around the old wooden table. An overhead light shines. Noses and lashes cast shadows on the faces. And then there is the crash. In the whirlwind of the aftermath, the father becomes newly aware of the flash of feeling that is his brief life. He goes to the store, starts crying in the cereal aisle, realizes the futility of his marriage, and falls in love with the checkout girl.

Imagining this, I stare down at the dog. His jaw, broken by the force of the boy's car, rests at an impossible angle. The boy has stopped gesturing and is just standing there, his head turned away from the dog, silently crying. Then he sobs, "My mother will kill me."

When I was younger, I used to have nightmares in which I would accidentally commit murder. Once I learned that I could kill by biting the inside of my cheek. At first I didn't believe it would really work and so I bit the secret spot while looking at a woman and she died. Afraid, I took off running. I was not upset that I had killed her; I was just afraid that everyone would find out.

I look at the boy. I look at my father. I look at the dog.

"Please don't tell her," the boy pleads. He hovers over the dead dog, his arm outstretched tentatively as if he might stroke it. The collar of my father's coat is partially tucked under itself, making a little ridge beneath the fabric on his shoulder.

"Okay, son—" I can hear him saying. "Just relax. We'll figure this out. We'll keep this between you and me." I raise my eyebrows to no one in particular and walk back inside the house to think about Ava.

Want led her to a precipice and it became too difficult to look behind or even forward beyond the will to have.

Ava's coveting unfolds, unfurls, becomes having. And the trouble with having is that it destroys the wanting.

In her car, foot on the gas, she shivers. The baby howls.

Where is she going to go? She has to vanish—but vanishing is a delicate thing. She can't afford to be a suspect. (It's a dismal combination—being both suspect and culprit.) Ava has watched her share of cable and knows that the police will question her.

Just then, my mother bangs into the house, through the front door. She is shrouded in words. Sharp nasal things that seem to emerge from her mouth like bees and cling to the air around her. I can't really hear what she's saying nor can I hear my father's responses. He walks into the kitchen and looks at me, then out the window again. His face registers that strange hope, then hope fades. He leaves the kitchen, my mother hurling the bees after him.

There are all kinds of ways to be pursued. Ava knows this. In a way, she's chased the baby. And now, in a reversal of wanting, the mother will chase her.

A door slams and my mother comes back to the kitchen table and throws herself into a chair. Her cheeks are flushed. "For God's sake," she says. "I married that man." She spears the cold fish on her plate and bursts into tears.

It has been this way between my mother and father ever since I can remember, but over the last few years, the trouble has intensified. They live in a giant disconnect, their marriage a barrel into which they pour their lost wants. I think the barrel has been quietly sinking, so heavy with its unspoken weight. But they have made a promise to leave it alone and now neither of them feels able to sift through its contents, dry off the brine, and see what's inside.

After my mother stops crying, we sit in a puddle of awkward silence. I am careful not to look directly at her.

Soon, I get up to go to the bathroom, leaving her sniffling above the cold fish. I stay in there for some time, not because I really have to go, but because there is this tightening in my chest, like the two sides of my ribs are being drawn toward one another by the turning of a knob in my spine. I look in the mirror and think about growing up in this house—looking into the mirror when I was a little girl and puzzling over the face that glowered back at me. My face. Something about it still catches me off guard.

After a while, there is nothing left for me to do. I have washed my hands and carefully lotioned them. I have checked my face for breakouts. I have held my hair up in various styles of ponytails to see how I look.

I head back to the kitchen.

"What happens to the nanny?" my mother asks, her eyes downcast.

"The story isn't done," I say. "I have to finish it."

"But you must know how it ends," she says.

"It is a terrible story," I say. "It won't end well."

"Good," says my mother.

Ava is in the car with the howling baby, her foot pressing on the gas, which now seems to her to be more than gas. It is a fuel of another magnitude, making more things run than just the car.

The baby shrieks and shrieks and all of Ava's muscles coil tightly around bone. She slows the car once she is on the highway. She doesn't want to get pulled over.

Miles fly by. The city turns into farmland. The sky opens and spreads. The baby, exhausted, falls asleep.

Ava has a plan. She turns around, drives home with the quiet baby, lays him on her quilt and curls around him to sleep. He wakes hours later, in the early morning, crying. She feeds him a bottle and he looks at her with his blank blue eyes and seems to forgive her.

The forgiveness in the baby's eyes—or at least the thing Ava perceives as forgiveness—is the first sign that she has truly transgressed.

She washes him with warm water in the bathroom sink and though she has seen his tiny stomach and toes many times during the time she has cared for him, she has never associated them with her future before. She makes a strange strangled sound and the baby looks up at her, vaguely alarmed. It's six-thirty in the morning. The dim, frail light of dawn filters through the window.

She loads the baby into the car. There is a mall in the next town over with a built-in day-care center. It opens early and she will drop him there. Then she will go to the mother's house as if to nanny the child that she knows is missing.

My mother looks at me. Her light brown eyes look tired and blank. I expect her to argue, to find something wrong with my story, but instead she just sighs, picks herself up, and begins to clear the table.

Her hands are aging. The blue worms of her veins have surfaced, making the skin above them look reptilian and thin.

I know that I should ask my mother if she is all right. She seems drained, red welts under her eyes. She walks from the table to the sink with the weight of a martyr. I'm grateful when she begins to run the sink.

I haven't lived in this house with my parents in over ten years. I come twice a year to visit and each time I feel even older, even more distant from them. But in some way, time has made us able to survive each other; we're all adults now. We understand the importance of leaving one another alone.

That morning, Ava shows up at the house the instant Katherine walks into the baby's room. Katherine stands, her dark hair tangled down her back, her face still puffy from sleep, and then she freezes. The realization creeps over her, a strange heat. She screams.

Then silence. Ava hears the scream from the driveway and for a moment forgets that she is the reason for it. She bounds up the steps and bangs on the door.

"Are you okay?" she calls through the door. Footsteps. The door swings open. Katherine's face is bloodless and Ava can tell that at this moment she is barely alive.

"Do you have him?" Katherine gasps.

You might imagine that Ava, again, is overcome. But somehow she feels nothing. In fact, she believes herself when she says, "Do I have who?"

"The baby," Katherine says, "Robert."

Robert. Ava hears his name and the image of those blank blue eyes overtakes her.

"He's not in his crib—He's not in the house—" Katherine flings herself about, calling his name. She opens closets, checks beneath furniture. Ava follows her, a worried shadow. Finally, the mother fumbles toward the phone and dials 911. She reports a missing baby, Robert Allen Hayes, stolen from his crib while he was sleeping. The nanny can only hear one side of the conversation but this is how she learns that the father of the child is responsible for the abduction. She hears Katherine tell the police that he has threatened to take the baby in the past, that he lives in Arizona and has a history of drug abuse. Ava feels her knees turn to jelly and goes into the living room to sit down.

Katherine comes in. For the first time, Ava feels tears welling in her eyes.

Katherine sits next to her for a minute, then she gets up and walks to the window, then she walks back to the couch and sits, then she stands and walks to the phone, picks it up, sets it down. Her hands are shaking.

Ava doesn't know what to say. Minutes pass, maybe fifteen, and the police arrive. They ask a lot of questions. Ava is pale, her tired face looks perfectly grief-stricken. The policeman leans in close to her hair when he questions her and Ava notices that he seems to be breathing her in. Normally, she would recoil at this type of advance. But today she understands that this is working to her advantage. She tells the policeman that she never met the father, that she has no information about the abduction, that she just came today to nanny and got caught up in the hurricane. She blinks her heavy lashes and a tear falls. The policeman hands her a Kleenex. She realizes that they must carry these little Kleenex packets along with their guns and billy clubs.

"Where were you last night?" the policeman asks, a suggestiveness to his tone. She widens her eyes and looks straight into his small brown ones.

"Home," she says to him.

He makes some notes on a little yellow pad and puts his large hand on her shoulder, gives it a little squeeze.

"I'll need your contact information," he says to her. She obliges.

"You're not going to let her get away with it, are you?" My mother asks this as if she already knows the answer and is disappointed.

"I'm not sure," I say.

My father is asleep in the living room. The television informs itself of the news as he snores.

"That wouldn't be right," she says. I'm sitting at the kitchen table clipping my toenails. The little slivers fall to the parquet floor. I imagine a flurry of toenails covering the wood, my parents tramping through the storm in big, woolly boots—

"Either she's overcome by guilt and confesses everything and returns the baby to the mother, or else she's caught. Maybe if she gets caught the mother and father will reunite..." My mother's voice drifts off after she says this. I try to determine if she is wistful or just distracted. It's impossible to say.

It's true that being slammed up against the possibility of loss might bring two estranged parents together. Realizing that he didn't steal the baby, Katherine might feel a wash of tenderness come over her—a profound desire to forgive those awful, siren-stained nights of cocaine and caving hopes. It would erase the memory of the strange way he used to smell when the drugs kicked in, like stale breath, metal, and fear. She would remember, instead, his knuckles, the way he ran his palm over her head, the easy and goofy way he laughed. She would allow herself to believe him when he said he was straight now and wanted to raise the child with her. She would look into his large, wet eyes and see her baby's eyes, the spread of her baby's broad face, and the casing that had hardened around her heart would turn to liquid and she would forgive him.

And such forgiveness leads to more forgiveness and a general generosity of spirit—and Katherine, in her newfound resolve to live in the present, would forgive Ava. The baby would grow up not remembering the episode, knowing only the two parents that love him.

I hate this ending. I look at my mother looking at her hands. She seems lost in a terrible thought, the swarm of bees inside her head now. She is mulling over something and I can tell it is dangerous, growing more powerful every time my father snores.

"I like that idea," I say to my mother. "I like the idea of a turn toward forgiveness." My mother's eyes brighten.

"Yes," she says. "It's a good one."

When I was young, we used to sit around the dinner table, the meat slightly wet-looking, a salad sitting perkily in a yellow bowl, and no one would speak. Those were the dinners I came to appreciate. Because if my mother did speak, my father would always respond with something one beat removed from the obvious point; my mother's jaw would tense, the clanking of her silverware growing louder like the music in an old movie.

"Do you listen?" she would ask him. "Or is that something people learn when they complete their dissertations—"

When my father met my mother, he had aspirations of becoming a classics professor but when I was born, in order to make ends meet, he got a job deep in the bowels of a university office. And the days passed fluidly by.

Whenever I witness one of their fights, two feelings rise inside me. On the one hand, I want to join in. I want to yell at both of them and expose how lazy and silly they are, have been, will be. I want to reveal their faults, hold their flaws under the living room's bright light, turn them over with a surgeon's precision, stun my parents into a better life. But another part of me wants to place a heavy, wool blanket over them both and mute the edginess that keeps slicing through the surface of things. The conflict of these two feelings usually leaves me knotted and silent, a tacit observer.

But lately it seems that my parents are aging in double time. The lines on my father's face are deepening at a remarkable pace and he seems to be growing smaller. My mother's anger has affected her posture. Her tense muscles are eating away at her, giving her less neck and a slight hunch to her back.

Today a new feeling adds itself to the conflict inside me. I feel a great, enveloping helplessness that is, I am aware, related to sadness.

I want to lean in and touch my mother but imagining the actual laying of my hand on her thin arm gives me the creeps. There is something in the air between us that I can't get through, though it seems I should be able to. Most daughters can probably grow sad in the presence of their mothers. The mutual empathy crackles between them: the mother, the daughter, the unspoken understanding. But this is a theoretical thing to me and I stay perfectly still.

Ava, overcome with fear, goes back to the day-care center, picks up Robert, and drives straight back to her apartment. He begins to howl again and this time she can't calm him with a bottle or running water. Panic threads through her. The telephone begins to ring. She puts him in the closet to deaden the noise and picks up the receiver.

I can't tell my mother that the parents won't reunite, that there will be no forgiveness, and this makes me feel deceptive. The dishes have been washed and put away, the counters scrubbed.

My mother has gone into the bedroom to read. I get up from the table where I have been thinking about the nanny and look in on my father who has awakened from his nap. He looks at me absently, his thinning hair tousled from sleep.

I once had a boyfriend, Ryan, whose mother was a manicurist. She did tiny little landscapes on her clients' fingernails. You could bring her a photograph, a postcard, and she would render the image perfectly. When Ryan was sixteen, he was cleaning out the garage and discovered old oil paintings she did in her youth. He found them overwhelmingly beautiful—deep color worked into the canvas, a looseness to the form. He urged his mother to paint again but she looked at him like he was crazy. "I paint every day," she told him. "I paint nails."

This reduction of hopes—from the canvas to the fingernail—occurred inside my father, as well. Only I've never been certain what his canvas was.

My father is a tall man, but sitting on the sofa, sunk into the cushions, he looks tiny. It probably has something to do with the pained look on his face. The childish hurt held captive beneath resignation. I want to say something to him.

"Sleep well?" I ask. He nods.

He stands and walks to the window.

In film, this would seem like a refrain. My father, the window. The window, my father. The window would be the portal, the symbolic opening to another world. Here, though, in this house, the window looks out onto the driveway which is speckled with the residue of oil drips. A large Douglas fir shades the view to the east and the house limits what you can see to the west. It's not a dingy urban window that reflects emotion, that refracts light, that makes you think of seedy desires and cheap vodka. It's not the glass pane set into a solitary log cabin deep in some mountain nook. It's a curtain-adorned, suburban window and my father's face is reflected along with the china cabinet and cheap, frosted chandelier. He looks out the window because it's there. Because it was built to be looked out of.

Back at her apartment that evening, the phone rings. With a trembling hand, Ava picks up the receiver. She croaks hello. It's as she feared. The police officer wants her to meet him at the station later for questioning. She prays he can't hear the baby's muffled sobs and gracefully acquiesces.

She hangs up, walks to the large glass doors of her apartment and looks out. Every telephone pole and city tree seems to sprout in the form of a question mark. She is a well of unanswerables.

She goes back into the kitchen and pours herself a glass of wine. She drinks it in big swigs. A slow heat glides through her and she tries to concentrate on its movement through her blood. There are so many problems in her mind that they drown one another out. A white noise. An indiscernible hum. And then, the realization that the baby is no longer crying.

Ava runs to the closet and flings open the door. His face is turned and he looks, to her horror, a strange shade of violet.

She grows faint. She clutches at him violently. She wants to shake the life back into his pudgy legs and arms, relocate the shards of forgiveness she had seen in his tiny baby eyes. What would be the point of her transgression if he died?

Her thoughts are bright red comets streaking past her vision. She can't keep up with them. And as her nails dig into his arms, he crinkles his brow and shrieks. She falls back, away from him, her blood speeding.

She sits on the sofa, calming the baby. It is easier than she anticipated. He seems to want to be calmed; he's drowsy. She puts her face against his tiny chest. He smells like a baby—diapers and new skin. Though she knows she has a long way to go, she feels victorious, blessed with luck. She looks at the his face. The pink in his cheeks seems to flower from his center and his lashes are delicate, almost silken. He looks like any normal baby: whole, peaceful, undisturbed. She picks him up, holds him to her chest, and walks into her bedroom. There, she stands before the mirror, staring at him, at herself, at the way they seem to blend into one entity.

My father is still looking out his window at the driveway. It seems that he has been waiting like this for years. As I watch him, I imagine him fading, growing dimmer until he is just the faintest outline of a body. Then he disappears. Though it is a depressing idea, it seems painless and I wonder if he is wishing for something similar.

My father never talks to me about my stories. If I tell my mother something in his presence, he gets a glazed look and begins to drift out to some large, luminous sea. I have always taken it as a passive acceptance of me, which is why it shocks me when he turns and says, "I think you're mother is right about your story." At this moment I feel alarm and shame, as if I have been caught doing something sexual in front of him.

"What?"

He shrugs. "I'm going to sleep," he says. "See you in the morning." I want to ask him what he means about my story, but I am so stunned that he was paying attention I can't think of a single thing to ask. Had he been listening all along? Or had he just heard my mother's upset voice as she instructed me on the dos and don'ts of my story?

It's not late, only eight o'clock. I want to leave this big, old house, its creaky walls and humming pipes, but there is nothing to do in town. I consider taking a walk around the neighborhood but the image of all the windows lit with bright, false light depresses me. I could cut over and sneak onto the golf course like I did when I was a teenager but now it just seems dangerous, no longer exhilarating.

I wipe some stray crumbs from the counter and look out the other window; it overlooks the same stretch of driveway. In the fading light of the autumn sky I can see a deer eating my mother's flowers.

I feel the onset of a headache and begin to wonder if I can change my flight and go home tomorrow, back to my cramped apartment in a bigger city. Back to my job and my bills.

I hear footsteps behind me and my mother comes in.

"Hi dear," she says and opens the refrigerator. She takes out the carton of milk and pours a glass. Without makeup she looks even more exhausted and slightly ashen. Her hair is down from its usual coil and hangs in haggard curls around her face.

My mother has always been thin, but with age she has grown frail. She's wearing a white nightgown with small light blue flowers on it and I try not to notice that I can see the lines of her body through the thin fabric.

The guilt I originally felt about withholding the real ending to my story has turned into self-doubt. At this point, I'm not even sure I want to tell the story at all.

My mother sets her milk on the table and sits. I walk over and join her. I wish I could tell her how old she and my father are becoming. That when I am with them the air gets harder to breathe. But I know these things are made up of that lethal powder we are born knowing not to use. So I sit there and watch her softening mouth close around the rim of her glass, the slight wiggle of the skin around her neck as she swallows.

Ava stands with the baby, the world a maze of avenues. She knows she will have to make a decision and that once she makes a move it will be final; there will be no turning back. The baby sleeps against her chest, lulled by her heartbeat. At some point he sighs. Ava closes her eyes, clutches him tighter, and realizes that many people live for just one such moment, when they are up against the thing they want most and no one can stop them.

After a brief stint as a federal investigator, Robin Romm decided to pursue an M.F.A. at San Francisco State University. She holds a B.A. in English and Creative Writing from Brown University. Her stories have appeared in *Threepenny Review*, *Northwest Review*, *Nimrod International*, *Five Fingers Review*, and other journals. She lives in Berkeley, Calif.